INCHINNAN PARISH CHURCH
SUNDAY SCHOOLS

WITH CHRISTMAS GREETINGS

December 1956

Vincent Kelly　　SCHOLAR

　　　　　　　　　TEACHER

John S. McIntail.　SUPERINTENDENT

DESMOND PLAYS THE GAME

BY

D. STAPLETON

W. & R. CHAMBERS, LTD.

LONDON AND EDINBURGH

Reprinted 1954

Printed in Great Britain at the Villafield Press, Bishopbriggs

CONTENTS

DESMOND PLAYS THE GAME.

CHAPTER I.

'SOME OLD GREEK BUSTS.'

'IT is a pity,' D'Arcy murmured, as he scanned the team-list on the table before him with mischievous black eyes, 'that this school, after teaching N. Desmond, Esq., how to knock out a man in the first round, how to swim a mile without gasping, how to run a mile without slacking, &c. &c., did not then teach him how to write. I tell you honestly, Tiger, I can't tell whether this is McLaren or Lestrange here——'

'Let's have a squint,' Telford murmured lazily, heaving himself out of the arm-chair in which he had curled himself while reading a novel. 'Jove, what a scrawl! Des doesn't half make a mess of things. I saw the Head staring at one of them in the passage once, and looking fit to explode. Des'll be doing copy before he's much older if he doesn't look out.'

'What does that matter? I bet this is Lestrange, anyhow. He always puts Les in when we play Wright's. I reckon we'll beat the rotters this time, Tiger.'

Telford swung upright, suddenly alert and frowning. 'Oh, hang it, Darkie, I hate it all.'

'All what?' D'Arcy raised his black brows, but he knew what Telford meant.

'This—business of running down Wright's. As if the School couldn't get on without all this inter-House bother. It wouldn't matter if it was the School House——'

'The School House!' D'Arcy spoke contemptuously. 'It's been left behind for years. Leigh's has been first for ages.'

'Oh, and if you belonged to Wright's you'd say the same about Wright's. As if they weren't as good as we are any day.'

'Tiger! What heresy! Better not let Des hear you.'

'Des thinks the same, I bet. He doesn't mind having a rise out of them or playing against them, but he said himself it was a bit off when we're playing School matches, and all the members of Leigh's call "Play up, Leigh's," and all Wright's call "Play up, Wright's," and between them they make enough din to drown the only house that calls for St Martin's—the School House. It's rotten hard on poor old Loring. After all, he's School-captain, but he's brushed aside in this endless bickering between Ranger and Rix.'

'Well, old Ranger's going.'

'Yes, but Rix isn't. And whoever's made captain of Leigh's instead of Ranger, he'll make it pretty hot for them. I should not like to be captain of Leigh's with dear Allerick in his present mood. It was that stunt of taking away their togs while they were bathing that finished him. An old trick, but effective. Jove, they weren't half-laughed at as they came over Smith's field!'

In spite of his avowed dislike for the inter-House feud, Telford laughed at the recollection of the dignified and scarecrow-like Allerick picking his way over the pasture, clad only in a bathing-suit, his brow thunderous.

'But you may be captain of Leigh's all the same——' began D'Arcy, but before he could finish his sentence the door opened and Ranger entered. He was a tall well-built fellow of eighteen, but perhaps he had been a little too irresponsible for the position he was now leaving. During his captaincy

the quarrel between Leigh's and Wright's
Houses had reached such a pitch that it
worried not only Loring, the School-captain,
but Mr Leigh, Mr Wright, and even the
Head-master, Dr Newton. From football
and swimming it had spread to cricket,
thence to forms and to the individual
members of each House, so from mere
boyish rivalry it had become a serious feud.
It became all a matter of 'paying out' and
'paying back,' and the School in general
was beginning to suffer from this pre-
occupation of each of the Houses with plots
against the other.

'If one House would let the thing drop,
the other would,' Loring said; 'but the
instinct to "get even" carries the affair on.'
But then no one listened to Loring.

Ranger came in now, half-smiling, and
gave D'Arcy a tremendous thump on the
back. 'I've given my official resignation
in, Darkie! It's all settled. Fetch the
flowers for my grave.'

'You're not sorry to go, are you?' Telford
asked, looking searchingly at him.

'Sorry? Who ever was sorry to go on a
world-trip with a rich uncle?' But Ranger's
laugh was a bit forced. He cared more for
St Martin's than his light-hearted manner

showed. 'I'm wondering who's going to be captain. I might say old Rix is getting his guns ready. I wonder if the old blighter'll say ta-ta to his little pal? We've had some good times together. I bet he wishes I was staying until they've got even with us for pinching their clothes.'

Telford stirred impatiently and drummed on the table with his fingers. He was a rather short untidy boy, with rough fair hair and serious grey eyes. His great aim was to get D'Arcy to treat life seriously. D'Arcy was tall, thin, and handsome, with gleaming eyes and black unruly hair. His smile was about as mischievous as anything could be, and even when his expression was serious his very voice seemed to smile. His nickname, which suited him so perfectly, had arisen out of a mistake of one of the Third form, who, when he first came to the School, read his name thus from the list of new boys. Desmond, then a pink little boy, with beautiful knees and infantile gaze, pounced on the pronunciation with great joy, and 'Darkie' D'Arcy remained ever since.

He laughed now as Ranger mentioned Allerick, and asked, 'Who do you think'll get the captaincy, Ray?'

'You,' answered Ranger.

'No dashed fear,' was D'Arcy's elegant rejoinder. 'The Head has too good a memory.'

'Oh well, he asked me if I had any suggestions, and I suggested you—that's all.'

'Did you?' D'Arcy flushed. 'Why not Des?'

Ranger shrugged his shoulders. 'Des takes life too seriously. He's not cut out for captain. Don't tell him I said so, of course —but——'

'He'd make a jolly sight better captain than you did!' hotly broke in Telford, for he never on any account heard a word against Desmond. 'He'd stop this nonsense about Wright's.'

'Feeling sore?' Ranger folded his arms and regarded the angry Telford as one might a yapping puppy. 'I know he would —that's why I didn't suggest him. Desmond is too noble, too forgiving——'

D'Arcy roared as if this were the best joke going, and continued, 'Too frail, too fragile, too angelic——'

'Too weak to battle with the storms of life——'

'Too small, too delicate——'

'You asses!' scoffed Tiger; 'there he is

coming,' as a firm footstep was heard along
the passage. Next moment the door, which
was already ajar, was kicked open with
some violence, and the subject of the
pleasant description entered. He was a six-
footer, and of Viking build, clear-skinned,
and brown-haired. His eyes were deep-set,
very dark blue, and absolutely fearless in their
gaze. The lift of his chin, the curve of his
mouth, and his walk were all arrogant, yet
his smile was so good to see that it made
even his conceit likeable. His voice was
very deep and gruff, as though he were used
to making it heard above many others, as
indeed he was. He came in now and
swung himself on to the table perilously
near the ink-well. ''Lo, you chaps!—Well,
Ranger, who's it to be?'

Ranger gave the others a quick glance,
and then, laying his hand on Desmond's
shoulder, answered, 'Congrats, old man.'

The flush which mounted to Desmond's
forehead made Ranger immediately regret his
poor joke. Desmond had evidently been
dreaming of being captain of Leigh's.

'I—I say——' he almost stammered, ' I——'

'He's pulling your leg,' Telford put in
hastily. 'You're not appointed. The Head
hasn't made a decision yet.'

'Oh——' Desmond's cheeks paled again. 'You'll die skitting, Ranger. I hope your uncle'll be able to take your feeble rises.'

'Sorry, Des,' said the graceless Ranger, for he suddenly realised that captaincy of Leigh's meant more to Desmond than to him, who had held it.

'Righto,' smiled Desmond. 'I'm not bursting to be captain, anyway,' he fibbed. 'Dare say it'll be old McLaren. Newton loves Mac.'

'Oh, my aunt! Mac! Save us from such a fate—I never thought of such a thing!' D'Arcy cried. 'We were thinking it would be either Lestrange or Palmer.'

'Or Darkie,' added Telford.

'Or me—yes,' repeated D'Arcy unblushingly.

'Are you going across to say good-bye to Rix?' questioned Desmond, turning to Ranger.

'I was just wondering,' smiled the captain. 'By the way, I met O'Shane in the quad, and the dear old bean sailed up to me. "So you're going already—R-r-ranger?" he said, with enough Antrim accent to cut a cheese. "Yes, little man; are you sorry?"—"Of course, Ranger! [With a broad beam.] Best of luck, and all that!"'

'O'Shane is a sport,' answered Desmond;
'and so is Rix, for that matter. We're apt
to underrate them while this quarrelling goes
on.'

'Just what I was saying!' added the Tiger
eagerly.

Ranger laughed. 'Oh well, I wonder if
Wright's say the same? Carry on, anyway,
you've got the field to yourselves. Are
you going to the lec? I'm not.'

'A lecture? What lecture?' questioned
the others.

'Mean to say you haven't seen the notice?
Jolly good job I mentioned it. It's up in
the porch there. At seven-thirty. On "Old
Greek Busts"—by the Head.'

'Oh help!' groaned Telford. 'Anybody
think I look pale? I think I've got a pain
or something.'

'No backing out,' grinned Desmond.
'Here, Tiger, hurry up and finish your
book; then you can lend it to me to read
over the lec. It's red, and there are such
things as red Bibles.'

'What cheek!' declared Telford. 'I've
only just started it. And, anyway, the old
Newt'd be pretty ratty if he caught you
reading even a Bible over his precious
lec.'

'Don't know — much more interesting,' answered Desmond. 'Well, what time is it, Ray?'

'Quarter to seven.'

'Jove! I've had nothing to eat since five,' Desmond said. 'I must get a bite.' He swung open the cupboard door and took possession of a piece of cake and some milk, of which he politely proceeded to partake.

'I suppose it's compulsory to go to the lec?' inquired the Tiger.

'Who'd go if it wasn't?' asked Ranger. 'It just says: "All members of the House are asked to attend in the chapel at seven-thirty"—that means we've got to be there.'

'Aren't Wright's going?'

'No. It's like that other lec on Latin that the Newt gave; he does one House at a time, so that he'll have the pleasure of giving the beastly thing three times.'

'I liked that Latin lec,' put in Desmond; 'it was jolly interesting.'

D'Arcy glared at him. 'Don't you feel well, Des?'

'Oh dry up!' answered Desmond sweetly. 'I can like the rotten lecs if I like—can't I?'

Telford picked up his book and stuck it in his torn blazer-pocket. 'I'll *aller*,' he

announced, 'and see what old Mac thinks.'
He departed to the next study, which he
shared with McLaren, at present writing
letters home to Ayr.

'Well, I'm not going to the lec, thank
Heaven,' murmured Ranger fervently. 'It'd
be too much to bear on a chap's last day
at School. I've got to pack if I'm going
to catch the nine-ten in the morning.'

'You won't, Ranger,' scoffed Desmond,
finishing his meal and banging the cupboard door—the only door he ever closed
quietly was the Head's, and that not always.
'You were never known to catch a train
promptly.'

'Oh yes—once,' declared Ranger. 'I recol-
lect, when I was an infant, going to a friend's
at Christmas, and there was going to be a
blow-out, and a Santa Claus. I was at the
station two or three hours too early.'

'Pure greed,' commented Desmond.
'Wasn't it, Darkie?'

'Rather,' agreed that gentleman. 'But
perhaps the same feelings'll drive him to-
morrow. Your uncle's rolling, isn't he?'

'He is, quite—literally and metaphorically.
Did I tell you he proposed giving a schol
to St Martin's? Don't worry, though, I'll
persuade him to change it to a new swimming-

baths. So long, you chaps! Call on me on your way back from the lec, and help to sit on the trunk, will you?'

'Righto,' simultaneously promised the others, and Ranger departed.

'The place 'll be rather different without old Ray, won't it?' said Desmond, selecting a pair of handsome tan shoes from the row in the cupboard and proceeding to don them in place of his gym-shoes.

'It will,' agreed D'Arcy; 'but no quieter if I can help it. I know one or two perfect larks, and I'll have a chance to try them now old Ray's gone. He never gave any-one else a chance.'

'Look here——' Desmond began.

'At your feet? Not worth it——' inter-rupted the graceless D'Arcy, for he knew exactly what protest Desmond was about to make.

'Shut up!' Desmond was fierce, not to be forestalled. 'Suppose you were made captain——'

'It isn't likely,' cut in D'Arcy again. 'I've too much reputation for——'

'Dash it! Will you be quiet?' asked Desmond, threatening him with a shoe.

'Oh, anything to oblige,' said D'Arcy with perfect smoothness. 'Carry on, carry on—keep calm—I wouldn't talk for the world when you want to tell me——'

'What are you doing now?'

'I was only——'

'Well, keep it till after. I want to tell you that if you're appointed captain your larks'll have to rip. We don't want them. Nobody wants them——'

'Wrong; I do,' broke in D'Arcy. Then seeing Desmond's expression, 'Oh, sorry— carry on—I'm dumb.'

'Wish you were, then——'

'What a chance it'd be for you, old man.' D'Arcy had decided to listen to no warnings, sermons, or good advice. They bored him. He rose suddenly, his dark eyes twinkling. 'Time to go to the lec, Des; we mustn't be late. Think how hurt the dear Newt would be.'

'Darkie——' Desmond made a final attempt.

D'Arcy suddenly snatched up the ink-well, and springing on to a chair beside Desmond, seized him by his hair, holding the ink-well above his neck. 'Shut up!' he roared. 'Do you hear? It's my turn now.'

'Oh, you're hopeless!' answered Desmond wearily. 'All right, come on. Where can I pinch a clean handkerchief from?'

By the time they were ready, after various
little arguments and fights, it was nearly
half-past seven, so they made their way
across the broad tiled quadrangle to the little
chapel, where they attended morning prayers,
Sunday services, and occasional instructive
lectures like the present one.

Most of the members of the House, about
fifty all told, were seated in the pews already,
talking in loud whispers, sniggering, bobbing
up and down, and occasionally throwing paper
pellets slyly across at each other.

Desmond and D'Arcy went to the back
pew, which was slightly higher than the
others—a mean trick!—where the Sixth sat,
to be able, or so it was said, to keep the
rest of the House in order. The other
prefects were already assembled there, and,
taken all round, they were a fine set of
fellows. McLaren, a scholarship boy, and
as poor as a church mouse, sat at the end;
he was a thick-set dour-looking boy of
middle height, not handsome at all, but
ugly, with a straightforward seriousness which
made him liked in spite of his lack of a sense
of humour. Lestrange was pale, thin, and
delicate, almost colourless in fact, except for
his wide grey eyes, in which there was a
dreamy expression. Perhaps no one would

guess on looking at his build that he was one of the best bowlers St Martin's had ever contained, but such was the truth.

Then there was Fendall, who was such a clever chap, always first at mathematics, and keen on trying experiments for himself, often with disastrous results, as the burn on his sunburnt cheek showed at the present moment. He was the dandy of the Sixth, ultra neat and fashionable, and the others were always making fun of his beautiful silk socks and startling blazers. He was very rich, and most generous—having a hand in all the big 'blow-outs' and 'treats' that went on at Leigh's, and heading all subscription lists with a big donation. Lestrange and he were hardly ever seen separately, such good chums had they been since the Third form, and as Fendall was as dark as Lestrange was fair, they made a startling and not unlovely contrast.

Next to Fendall, his long legs stretching well under the seat of the pew in front, was Palmer—an extremely nervous boy, with a very small head crowned with ugly red hair. He wore horn-rimmed spectacles; and it was rumoured that he wrote poetry, although, as he was a very decent chap when one knew him, none of his fellows sought to lay the

awful sin to his charge, and any odes, epics,
or lyrics which he might have written were
carefully hidden. Palmer hardly ever spoke
to anyone except Waugh, his study-mate;
and even Waugh, who was on the plump
side and decidedly ruddy, could hardly boast
of long conversations with his chum.

Horton, centre-forward in the First Eleven,
and of formidable height and build, was
possessed of a fierce temper, and an obstinate
self-righteousness. He it was more than any
other member of the Sixth who helped to
make serious the quarrel between Leigh's
and Wright's. According to Horton, everything Leigh's did was right, everything
Wright's did was wrong. He would not
speak to a member of the other House if he
could help it, and he would not have smiled
at them on pain of death. On the day
when he slipped and twisted his ankle
coming across the playing-fields, O'Shane
had courteously offered his arm to help him
to his feet, and Horton had swept the kind-
ness aside with a growl like an angry dog.
O'Shane had merely smiled and stared after
the other, his Irish blue eyes twinkling.

Sikes, the last member of the Sixth, shared
study with Horton, and was so afraid of the
latter that he was entirely under the fellow's

thumb. Sikes had two hobbies, stamp-collect-
ing and bug-hunting, and he was always
'swapping' a particularly interesting beetle
for a stamp some other chap had and which
he envied, and afterwards regretted the trans-
action. From this his character may be
inferred, he hardly knew his own mind for
two seconds together. If Horton praised
anyone up, he agreed with Horton; if somebody spoke against the same person, he
agreed with him also. Therefore, because
Horton persecuted Wright's, Sikes followed
him, though he admired Allerick, and was
positively attracted by O'Shane.

'Funny of the Head to be late,' said
Desmond, as he took his seat.

'Perhaps he's forgotten to turn up,'
answered D'Arcy hopefully, for Dr Newton
was sometimes a little absent-minded.

'Too good to be true!' retorted Desmond.
'He never forgets lectures or canings, though
he may forget half-hols or such-like.' He
did not speak seriously, for the Head-master
was far from being unpopular.

The audience was getting distinctly impatient
by ten to eight. All the spare hymn-sheets
had been made into pellets and used, and the
juniors had almost all performed the daring
feat of walking through the pulpit where the

on the verge of a smile. No wonder St Martin's loved him to a man! But they feared him too. When he was near any of them they were filled with admiration, and faint praise from him was more acceptable than the highest appreciation of other masters.

'Well, Desmond?' He smiled now, showing his most beautiful white teeth. The slight scar running beside his lip that was a memento of Gallipoli was now visible, without spoiling the smile, however.

Desmond flushed. His flush was one of his greatest trials, it was quick and vivid as any girl's, mounting up from his throat to his rough brown hair. 'I came to say— we're all waiting, sir,' he began lamely. 'I thought, perhaps——'

'Waiting?' Weird conjectures fluttered across the Head-master's brain. His smile faded. 'What do you mean, Desmond?'

'Er—the lecture, sir,' Desmond was stammering; 'we have been there since half-past seven——'

'Where, Desmond?'

'In the chapel, sir.'

'And what lecture is this?'

Only then did Desmond begin to suspect a hoax. 'A lecture on "Some old Greek busts," sir.' He realised as he answered that the title of the lecture was an extremely silly sentence.

'Some old Greek—I beg your pardon, Desmond?'

For the life of him Desmond could not say 'busts' again. 'On statues, sir.' He knew now that it was a joke, and his face became scarlet.

For a moment the Head stared in silence, then suddenly his smile broke out. He waved his long-fingered sunburnt hand towards the chair. 'Sit down, boy,' he ordered. 'I must hear about this. Tell me from the beginning.'

Desmond sat down, and began to cool down a little. 'There is a notice—or there *was* a notice, sir, on the board behind the hall door: "This House is requested to attend in the chapel at seven-thirty, Wednesday, when a lecture is to be given by Dr Newton on——"'

'Yes, yes—I see.' The Head did not wish the 'old Greek' to 'bust' again. 'Yes, Desmond. I didn't put it there. I wonder who did?'

Desmond was silent, considering the austere pattern of the thick carpet. He knew all the same, as surely as he sat there, that it was the revenge of Wright's House. And he knew also that the Head had few doubts

on that score. The meanness of it! The
low-down caddishness! He had to clench
his fists to conceal the anger within him.
Then looking up he caught the deep eyes
of the Head-master fixed upon him. 'Well,
Desmond,' he continued. 'I'll tell you what
I'm going to do'—the enthusiastic way in
which he said this sentence made him seem
surely the youngest and most boyish Head
in existence, and yet his expression was so
stern!—'I'll just leave it with you. The
inventor of the practical joke—for such, of
course, it is—was probably counting on your
coming to me, so let's just pretend you
didn't, eh? Pretend I sent for you. Not,
of course, that it wouldn't have been the
right thing for you to come and give me a
gentle reminder if I had forgotten to turn
up at a lecture. But I don't think I should
forget. Don't try not to smile, boy. I know
you don't care for my lectures, and you think
them dry. But some day, perhaps, you'll be
glad you listened—or didn't listen—to them.
Things good for us aren't always pleasant.'

Desmond smiled. Never before had he
liked the Newt so much. 'Thank you, sir,'
he answered, and half rose.

'No—sit still, Desmond; it won't do those
boys any harm to stay quiet in the chapel

for a while longer.'—Desmond had a momentary glimpse of the paper pellets and hymn-sheets, and doubted the 'quietness.'—'Stay, though, I'll send word to them. I must talk to you a while. Sit back on the chair, boy, and don't look so uncomfortable. Anyone would think you were afraid of me.'

His words amounted to an order, and Desmond, more flushed, if possible, than ever, tried to look as if he were lolling in the study of a boy-friend. It didn't act very well, however. The Head rang the bell, and Seddon, the butler, appeared. 'Go to the chapel, Seddon, and tell the gentlemen there that there is to be no lecture. Thank you.'

Seddon, silent and straight, slipped through the heavy door like a shadow. Dr Newton turned to Desmond again. 'I would have sent for you in any case, Desmond, to tell you that I have decided to appoint you captain of Leigh's House.' He paused to let the news sink in.

Desmond paled now, then the colour surged back in a wave of rapture. Captain of Leigh's! Captain of Leigh's! The title seemed to throb in his brain. He was so proud that he felt never again would there be a moment like this.

Dr Newton watched his expression—finding, somehow, a peculiar pleasure in contemplating this glorious example of English youth. Perhaps he remembered how he, too, had been captain of his House, and considered it the greatest thing in life—long ago, it seemed, before the curse that was the War descended. Perhaps it was some such memory that made his voice colder than ever as he said, 'Before all the glorious possibilities of such a position crowd in on your brain, Desmond, I should like you to see one matter from the point of view of the School. That is, this strange and growing enmity between the members of Mr Leigh's House and those of Mr Wright's.'

'Yes, sir.' Desmond was alert again at once. This last insult to Leigh's was more than bearable. Something must be done. Especially now he was captain of Leigh's and the House was his responsibility. He looked the Head directly, hopefully, between the eyes. How good it was to have such a man for a Head-master! There was no working in the dark—everything was open and above-board. Whatever mistakes he was going to make at his post in the future, Desmond was going to start right.

You see, Desmond,' continued Dr Newton,

'that it isn't only a case of having fun. Nobody wants you to enjoy life more than I do. You should be happy at such a time and in such a place. The joy of life is a legacy handed down by even those of this very School—not much older than you, Desmond—who gave themselves for the clean and worthy traditions which they loved.' For a moment, being a contemporary of those to whom he referred, the Head played with an ivory paper-knife on the desk before him, balancing it between his fingers as he gazed, lost in thought, at the bust of Dante Alighieri on the corner of the desk.

Desmond waited, wishing impatiently that the Newt would cut the sermons and carry on. It wasn't Armistice Day, and it was hardly fair to make a chap hear the thing twice.

As though he divined the boy's thoughts, the Head-master suddenly cast away the paper-knife and straightened his shoulders. 'But about this affair. It isn't mere fun. I've watched, boy, and I see more than most of you think. You probably suppose that when you are doing anything against rules it's a case of "Cave—the Head," and I know nothing of it. Now I never believed in a Head-master spying on his School, but neither am I convinced that it is right for him to accept the reports of his Staff without trying to verify them and form his own opinions of the different characters under his rule. I want to know every boy who comes to St Martin's, and I blame myself if I forget, even momentarily, the name of one boy. I'm letting you into my heart a good bit, Desmond, but that's because you're captain of Leigh's.' His quick smile won its response from the boy's intent face and died into sternness again. 'Therefore I hate to think that there is anything which keeps this School from being the great and united power it could be. And if there is one thing which stands in the way of its high purpose, in the way of all its achievements at work and play, it is this unaccountable, unending, ridiculous quarrel between the two Houses. . . . When did it commence?'

'I can't remember, sir. Nobody seems to know who started it.'

'Well, who's going to end it? I've met quarrels between Classic and Modern, Arts and Science Houses before, but never one like this. It has become such an obsession that even the School House is affected. It is rifting into the supporters of Wright's and the supporters of Leigh's.'

Desmond had nothing but admiration for the way in which the Head had seen into the inner workings of the School.

'This mustn't happen. You must stop the thing, Desmond. We must have *esprit de corps*, not party feeling, at St Martin's. Henceforth I am merciless on anyone who does anything to carry on the foolish feud. And I am looking to you to help. I know I can trust you.'

He said nothing about the other members of either House—not even Allerick, Desmond noticed; but that was like the Head of St Martin's, he never judged one boy to another.

'I'll do everything I can, sir, I promise,' Desmond answered, and indeed he would have promised anything for the Newt at this minute. But such a promise—why, he had always disliked the affair, even when engaging in some priceless 'stunt' against Wright's—for Desmond had his share of blame, you may be sure, and plenty of it, when he had been in the Fifth, and less dignified.

'Don't be too sure or too hasty, boy,' the Head gave as his parting advice. 'Get the others in the Leigh part of the Sixth with you first. Remember you're captain, but act quietly. That's all.'

Desmond went out from the strange interview with a curious elation. Here were fields to take and battles to win. In his mind he saw the feud already ended, and the two Houses united, himself and Allerick strolling round the playing-fields together. At the thought of Allerick, however, he frowned. He must go warily with Rix.

As though his thought became personified, Allerick himself turned the corner of the passage, and the two boys—the two *captains*, Desmond reflected, flushing deeply again— came face to face. Allerick was carrying a pile of books. He was about to glare at Desmond and pass on, or even to make some biting comment about the lecture hoax, when he noticed the curious phenomenon that Desmond was smiling. It was so long since a member of Leigh's had smiled at him, apart from spite or derision, that Allerick nearly dropped his books. But there was nothing either spiteful or derisive about Desmond's smile.

'Allerick,' said Desmond.

Allerick paused, alert and wary, the smile was *too* strange after Leigh's had just been taken in so beautifully. Allerick was an ugly boy, being very thin and bony. His hair was like dark tow, it seemed impossible that it had ever been combed. He possessed a receding chin, and his skin was dark, his ears large. His only beautiful feature, a pair of large dark-brown eyes, were successfully hidden by thick horn-rimmed glasses, known in St Martin's as 'Harold Lloyds.' Moreover, clever though Allerick undoubtedly was, he had not yet learnt the art of consideration for the foibles and fancies of his fellows. He was blunt of speech, direct, sudden, speaking exactly what came into his mind without tact or mercy. O'Shane and Hare and a few others of Wright's had discovered the goodness of heart behind all his rough speech, but others, less intelligent or less patient, called him boorish, or even 'Rough Rix'—for the sake of alliteration.

'Well?' he answered Desmond without returning the smile.

Desmond was overcome by a sudden attack of nerves. Rix was no easy person to approach. His glance fell to the pile of books in Allerick's arms. 'Can't you dump these down somewhere?' he said. 'I—I'— he could have kicked himself for stuttering— 'I want to jaw to you for a sec or two.'

Allerick's expression called Desmond mad. 'Jaw?' he burst out. 'To me?' Then with unveiled suspicion, 'See here, what's the game?'

'There's no game,' Desmond answered quietly. 'I say, Allerick, do forget for a moment I'm a Leigh's chap—or at least forget you hate Leigh's, and talk sanely.'

'What about? You can't get a rise out of me, Desmond. I'm an old hand.'

'How can I speak to you at all if you will persist in thinking I want to get a rise out of you? Why should I? It's you who've just got a rise out of us, isn't it? Don't you see I'm serious when I can come to speak to you to-night?'

'You didn't,' snapped Allerick. 'You met me.'

'But I would have come. I say, Allerick, let's get in your study; I bet your arms are aching.'

Desmond looked at Allerick steadily. Allerick returned the gaze, studying the other with perhaps a little envy. Then he turned aside and, without another word, led the other to the study which he shared with O'Shane. The Irishman was there now, wallowing in whitening as he cleaned his own and Allerick's gymnasium-shoes. It was a duty he would never assign to Pindle-thwaite, their fag, not only because 'Piffle' was a little grub, and couldn't clean anything properly, but also O'Shane loved doing it himself. He had put several coats on the shoes, enough almost to have whitened those of the whole school, while there was a large daub of dried whitening on his cheek, and a small portion of the block of cleaner on his hair.

O'Shane was from the north of Ireland, a place of mist and smooth air; he was tall, thin, and lithe. His eyes were as blue and twinkling as stars; and when he smiled, his thin-lipped mouth seemed to stretch from ear to ear in one great curve of joy beneath his high sun-tanned cheek-bones. And he often smiled, for things which were big troubles to other fellows lay light as thistle-down on O'Shane. Moreover, he was the same everywhere and with everyone. No one ever heard him say he disliked another chap.

He looked up now as the two came in, and any astonishment he felt in seeing Desmond with his friend was swept from his face by a welcoming smile. ''Lo, Rix, old man.— How do, Desmond? 'Fraid I've got all the chairs.' His voice was extraordinarily sweet, and no amount of education could take out of it the soft up-lilt that was his heritage. He hastily snatched one or two of the cleaning instruments from the surrounding chairs and departed to the corner.

'Now,' said Allerick to Desmond, dumping his books on the table and then swinging himself up beside them, 'out with it!'

Desmond was at a loss how to begin. O'Shane, looking up again, caught his expression, and cut in, 'I say, am I one too many? I'll buzz off——'

'No; it's quite all right,' began Desmond. But Allerick said curtly, 'Right, Pat. Desmond's not going to be long, though,' he added—causing O'Shane to smile at Desmond as much as to say, 'Don't mind him. We know what he's like,' as he vanished round the door.

In spite of his sincere liking for O'Shane, Desmond was glad that he had gone. 'I've been made captain of Leigh's,' began he.

'Oh!' Allerick said, starting. Then he added very dryly, 'Congratulations.'

'And what I've come to you about is this beastly bickering that's always going on between Wright's and Leigh's. I hate it, and I want it to stop.'

Perhaps it was a bad way to put it. It

was asking for Allerick's answer: 'Oh, and you think it 'll stop just because you want it to?'

Desmond let the taunt pass. He was hot-headed enough to resent it, but he was keeping his own feelings in the background, still under the influence of the interview with the Head. 'Not exactly,' he continued calmly. 'But I 'm captain of Leigh's, and you 're captain of Wright's, and if we both wanted it to stop, it *would sometime.*'

Allerick was affected at last. Desmond knew this by the savage way in which he kicked at the table-leg. Then suddenly he looked up, his eyes serious. 'Do you mean that, Desmond?'

'Rather!' said Desmond eagerly. 'Look here, Allerick; you *do* hate this messing, don't you?'

'I do!' answered Allerick heartily, 'as much as anyone. But, hang it, Wright's can't go on letting Leigh's rag them. We must hold our own.'

'Leigh's might say the same. And, as old Loring says, that 's what carries——'

'It wasn't that with Ranger,' Allerick broke in; 'he loved the fight for fighting's sake. He was——'

'Let 's leave Ranger out of it,' Desmond

in his turn interrupted. 'He's going. I'm captain. If I do all I can to stop the Leigh's versus Wright's—will you?'

'Like a shot!' agreed Allerick. 'Here's my hand on it. And remember, it's yours to act now. We scored with the lecture stunt, so——'

'It'll be as right as rain,' Desmond answered with the optimism of success, for never in his wildest dreams had he imagined such a change as he now saw in Allerick.

'Here's my hand on it!' Allerick said, springing from the table. 'We're in fair fight; you've got to win over Leigh's, I've to win over Wright's. Care to stay and have some supper with Pat O'Shane and me?'

'I'd jump at it,' smiled Desmond, 'only I must get back. The fellows over there haven't heard of my appointment yet. I was just coming from the Head when I met you.'

'I see. I'll knock on the wall for Pat.'

But in answer to his knock, Gregory as well as O'Shane entered from the next study. Gregory was one of the hottest persecutor's of Leigh's, and he nearly collapsed when he saw Desmond there. Desmond did not care for Gregory, but in the glow of his new resolution he smiled at him and said, 'Hullo, Gregory!'

Gregory had no answering smile for the visitor. The remembrance of the pebbled beach and the unclothed feelings of the day before made him too bitter against Leigh's. He gazed at Desmond as though he were some poisonous reptile, then with a look at the other two as much as to say, 'How on earth could you?' he turned on his heel and marched out.

Desmond laughed lightly in spite of his own resentment. 'Ah well! One can't blame the little man, perhaps.—Well, so long, Rix!' It was the first time he had called Allerick by his nickname to his face. 'Cheerio, O'Shane, old man!' He went. The asphalted quadrangle which lay between the two Houses seemed like air beneath his feet. He entered Leigh's porch as if he owned it, his head thrown back with fierce pride. Now to break the news to D'Arcy and the rest! . . . Captain of Leigh's!

CHAPTER III.

A MISUNDERSTANDING.

DESMOND awoke next morning from dreams of cricket and swimming to the glorious importance of being captain of Leigh's. All sorts of wonderful possibilities floated across his brain as he gaily splashed about in cold water until he was drenched and glowing. Hurriedly he dressed and left his small bed cubicle, more eager to get to his study than he could ever remember being before. He was surprised to find D'Arcy— lazy and bed-loving D'Arcy—sprawling on the couch reading.

'Hullo!' cried Desmond. 'What on earth's happened? Did you mistake the time?'

'No,' D'Arcy grinned. 'Did you?'

'No,' Desmond said. 'It's a quarter to seven. But, my hat, Darkie, whatever got *you* up before rising bell?'

'A wheeze,' replied D'Arcy, and began to chuckle softly. 'Rejoice, friend, we are revenged. *Per se!* Alone I did it!'

Desmond's eager young face grew suddenly

hard, and a fear entered his brain. He strode up to the couch, suddenly stern. 'What have you been up to, Darkie?' he demanded.

D'Arcy sat up. 'Why the strong man look?' he inquired. 'Anyone'd think I'd done something to annoy you.'

'Oh, stow that; I want to hear about this "wheeze" you're so joyous over.'

'Oh, Des, it's simply perfect! I thought of it just as I went to sleep last night, and the thought of it woke me up this morning! It's priceless! Now or never, I thought. You know that Lord Inverslowe —the Head's little pal?'

'Yes, yes,' answered Desmond impatiently.

'Well, he's keen on collecting things, and he's going to show us all his priceless collection of coins—the stuffy old bird——'

'Yes, Darkie, I know—get on with the "wheeze."'

D'Arcy gazed at his friend's worried face in amazement. 'Anyone'd think you'd lost sixpence. Well, this Inverslowe's going round Wright's this afternoon to see that daft old museum they've got in their library. So I knew dear Allerick and the rest would be round this morning getting the place all dressed up——' He broke off to chuckle again.

Desmond's heart sank lower and lower.

'All right, stop that crowing and go on,' he snapped.

'So I thought I'd help. I was up soon after six—heroic martyr in a great cause—and nipped up to their library through the side door, having packed a small attaché-case with the necessary equipment. Oh, Des, Des, you should see it! I thought of telling you, but I suddenly remembered that you were captain, and you might have qualms, old boy, and I didn't want your beastly conscience to suffer——'

'Oh, for goodness' sake, tell me what you've done!'

'Keep your wool on; it's a perfectly lovely rag. First I removed all the labels from the exhibits, or nearly all—I hadn't time to do the thing as thoroughly as I wished. Some I just swopped over, as for instance, on that stodgy bust of Cæsar, I put "Fossil found in North Wessex"—and so on. But where I could I made new labels. You know that awful ratty-looking Chinese god with all the teeth and the ten waving arms?'

'Yes,' answered Desmond, unsmiling and intent.

'Well, on that I put "Portrait of Mr B. D. Allerick watching Leigh's win the Shield Final."'

A gleam lit Desmond's eyes involuntarily for a moment, then died into sheer horror. 'Oh, Darkie!' he groaned. 'You awful ass! I could kill you!'

D'Arcy stared, then theatrically he pulled his blazer open and threw back his head, with closed eyes. 'Strike on!' said he. 'I die by a comrade's hand!'

But Desmond took no notice, he was pulling at his hair, as he always did when he was worried. 'I wonder if there's time?' he fumed. 'We must get it straight again!'

'What?' D'Arcy sprang to his feet as if stung. 'What's that? Get—it—straight again! Do you mean to say——'

'I mean to say,' broke in Desmond, cooling down a little and gripping D'Arcy's shoulder, 'that you've made a hash of things by this trick, Darkie. But it's partly my fault. I should have told you last night that Rix and I had called quits——'

D'Arcy's face became, if possible, more astonished than before. 'Called quits! What on earth for? Rix!'

'Because this beastly affair has gone far enough. I said Leigh's would forget about the lecture business and that'd be the end. We shook hands on it. And now——'

'I see.' D'Arcy grasped the situation at last. 'Well, how was I to know, Des? I thought you'd be fairly in stitches over the wheeze. It's too late to put the old museum straight now, anyway,' he added, with not altogether sad conviction; 'but I might go and explain things to Rix.'

'Don't be an ass. How can you? What's done's done.' Desmond threw himself disconsolately into an arm-chair.

D'Arcy began to look quite alarmed. 'I say, Des, I didn't know you took this business to your jolly old heart. Cheer up, face. We've still a chance. Wright's will pay us back, and *then* we can do the suffering hero stunt. It would have been a pity to waste such a good wheeze.'

The cloud on Desmond's face cleared for a moment, then came again. 'Don't you believe it,' he answered. 'Allerick'll never trust us again. They'll be so mad. They think there's nothing on earth like their old museum. Oh crumbs, and I thought I'd settled things!'

'Let's go across and explain,' suggested D'Arcy. 'If they haven't seen the place yet they might listen.'

'There's the rising-bell,' said Desmond. 'Somebody's bound to see it before we could get to them. And I believe *Rix* is always up before the bell. No, we'll just have to face things out. Never mind, Darkie.'

'I'll go and get old Tiger out of bed,' said D'Arcy; 'he never gets up of his own accord.' He gave a half-ashamed glance at his friend's dejected attitude, and went out whistling loudly.

As soon as he had gone, Desmond straightened himself up, settling his shoulders as though for battle. No use sitting worrying! Something would have to be done. He opened the study window and vaulted lightly on to the tennis-courts outside, then he ran as quickly as he could across the quadrangle to the porch of Wright's House. Just as he reached the long glass door it was opened, and he found himself face to face with Allerick.

Allerick's face was such a study of rage and humiliation that Desmond remained frozen to the spot. When he opened his mouth to speak at last, the captain of Wright's was before him. 'This is about the last straw!' the latter said. 'You come grinning to me about peace and good-will just to put me off the track while you carry out a rotten trick like this.'

The disgust in Allerick's voice whipped the

rich colour into Desmond's cheeks again. In
spite of himself, he felt his quick temper
rising.   Allerick had jumped to the conclusion
so hastily, had denounced Desmond's hand-
shake with such assurance. 'Wait, Allerick,'
he interrupted, 'I want to explain. I didn't
know——'

'Explain?' Allerick clenched his fists, his
voice rising. 'Isn't the mess you've made
of that show explanation enough? Won't it
be explanation enough for the Head and
Lord Inverslowe? Bah, you rotten sneak——'

'Allerick!' Desmond's eyes blazed. 'How
dare you——'

'Dare? I'd dare more than that—that,
for instance.' Allerick's arm shot out, and
he smacked Desmond's flushed face with his
open palm.

Desmond was up in arms at once. He
answered the smack with a lunge at Allerick's
chin. Allerick stepped quickly aside and, as
Desmond came forward, he caught him a
sharp blow on the mouth, knocking him
backwards. Desmond scrambled for his feet,
and the blood began to run down his chin
from his loosened teeth and cut lip. He
saw Allerick taking off his coat, and his own
hands went to his blazer. Then it swept
across his mind that he was captain of

Leigh's and Allerick was captain of Wright's, and they were fighting like two noisy fags. With a new determination he straightened his shoulders, his hands dropping to his sides. 'We can't fight, Allerick,' he said coldly.

'Can't fight? Are you going to cry off because you were getting the worst of it?'

Allerick strode forward, and for a moment it seemed that he would strike Desmond again; but he turned aside with a gesture of unbounded contempt. 'You make a fitting captain for Leigh's!' he said, and suddenly went into the hall, closing the door sharply behind him.

Desmond stood looking after him for quite two minutes, and a more striking contrast to the hopeful and proud figure of the night before could hardly have been imagined. His head ached from Allerick's blow, and his lip was swelling rapidly. As he turned to make his way back to Leigh's the prayer bell rang, and he hurried to bathe his lip. The study was empty, but as he came out again into the passage to the hall he met D'Arcy and Telford.

'Hullo! What's up?' cried Telford, noticing the swollen lip at once. 'Been fighting?'

'Looks like it, doesn't it?' cut in D'Arcy,

never guessing the truth. 'Been trying conclusions with old Rix after all?'

'Yes,' Desmond answered curtly, finding a rather morbid amusement in their astonished expressions.

'I say, Des——' began D'Arcy.

But Desmond would not let him continue. 'I met him, and he was feeling a bit—hurt —about the museum, that's all.—Did you hear of Darkie's ingenuity, Tiger?'

'I did,' answered the Tiger grimly. 'He appreciated all my happy laughter, I'm sure, but I let him know he should have consulted us.'

'I'm wasted on this School,' D'Arcy grumbled. 'First Des, and then you, snapping my head off when I was so happy in my good deed. There's too much peace and loving-kindness all of a sudden.'

Desmond touched his lip tentatively. 'Yes; I've just experienced some,' he murmured. 'Well, Darkie, don't do such a thing again, that's all. Things are going to be jolly difficult, I'm afraid.'

'Cheer up, you're captain of Leigh's, anyway,' smiled Telford, who had a tactful way of seeing the bright side.

Desmond's head went up a couple of inches. 'Yes, I am captain,' he replied quietly, as they entered the chapel and he took his place at the end of Leigh's Sixth-form row.

But even the thought of his honourable position could not wholly lift his despondency at the turn events had taken. It was all he could do to restrain his anger against the nonchalant D'Arcy. He gazed at Dr Newton as he read the morning Scripture portion, and mentally registered a vow not to give in, or to slacken his energies, till the breach between the two Houses was mended, though both the Houses were against him. Perhaps it was only his fancy, but he thought that in the prayers the Head-master spoke his appeal that the School might be 'united for service' with extra emphasis. Desmond half-opened his eyes and raised his head a little. Just above the top of the reading-desk he could see the Head's shining dark head, his long brown fingers clasped on the oak. It was worth doing anything for a hint from a man like that. Then Desmond turned his head to the three long lines belonging to Wright's House. At the end of the first was the ugly Allerick, his coarse hair appearing like a brown thistle as he bent. Desmond's hand went up to his aching jaw, then suddenly he smiled, and sang 'Amen' with extra fervour, though he had heard very little of the prayers that morning.

'Before you dismiss, boys,' said Dr Newton, smiling round on them as though his smile were specially for each one of them, 'I have a very pleasant announcement to make. Lord Inverslowe, my old school-friend who is staying with me for the week-end, kindly promised to show the School his collection of old European coins. He has, however, formed such a high opinion of the intellect here, that he has even decided upon a further honour for you. As some of you probably know, he went to Mexico last autumn for the purpose of excavating a wonderful old buried city there. On this excursion he obtained priceless and highly valuable relics of pottery, jewellery, and coins. These, as well as the other collection, are to be displayed in the library this afternoon at three o'clock. I would like the School to proceed in single orderly file through the right door and out of the left. Lord Inverslowe will stand beside the long table on which his collection is to be arranged, and answer any questions about it. I would like you to ask his permission before handling any of the exhibits. It is a wonderful opportunity, boys, and I am sure that you will appreciate it. Good-morning, boys. Dismiss.'

'What a rotten bore!' Robson said to his companion, Hare, as they left the chapel. 'Why, I've seen collections in every part of the world. I suppose it's all right for chaps who've not travelled and seen all the leading museums; but I think the Head ought to discover who they are, and not just order everyone to go.'

'I don't remember him doing any ordering at all,' replied Hare.

Hare, disrespectfully known as 'Whiskers,' was a rather short dark boy, quiet, and almost retiring. He was known as a bookworm, because he always swotted hard for examinations; but he was also in the Second Eleven, and a not undistinguished batsman. He had steady grey eyes, and a way of saying things which left you rather undecided as to whether he was serious or sarcastic. He smiled now at Robson, considering the rich fellow's bearing with a humorous tolerance.

Robson, the richest boy at St Martin's, was a problem even to Hare's far-seeing mind. He had come into the Fifth form eighteen months ago, and all fellows knew was that he hailed from America and had apparently money to burn. His handsome appearance, brought about by shining, very fair hair, strong features, and a splendid physique, were marred by the superciliousness of his continual cold half-smile and the arrogance of his bearing. His mention of the 'castle— our yacht—our little park in Sussex,' and so on, were merely put down to swank by Wright's, yet he was certainly not all affectation and empty-headedness. Out of his grey eyes at times there came a peculiarly swift and piercing glance, sometimes like a menace, to be veiled again by the contemptuous smile. 'What rot! You must be deaf, then?' he asserted now. 'Didn't he order us to go through the library in a beastly single file?'

'No,' replied Hare. 'He said that he *would like* us to do so.'

'And do you mean to say that that, coming from the Newt, is not an order?' demanded Robson.

'Of course. How can it be? Anyway, Robbie, don't be so superior. Every chap hasn't had your chances. What I wouldn't give for a sail round the globe!'

Robson laughed rather affectedly. 'If we go off on our jolly old yacht again, I'll get the pater to invite you,' he said lightly.

'That would be fine,' Hare replied. 'Perhaps you thought I was hinting?'

'No; rather not, Whiskers.'

'I'm sure your yacht must be perfect,' Hare said. 'Swimming baths, library, tennis-courts, croquet, and everything.'

'Oh, rather!' replied Robson complacently. 'All the modern improvements.'

'Makes you unable to understand those fellows who prefer to tramp round Scotland and Wales with an old stick and an ordnance survey map and a canvas bag, doesn't it?' Hare rattled on, only his eyes not remaining serious.

'Oh, of course, that's simply too bourgeois, I should think.'

'Quite too bourgeois,' Hare answered. 'I say, Desmond looks as if he had got toothache.'

'Serve the fellow right,' Gregory, who drifted up at this moment, declared. 'Do you know, the fellow was round calling on Rix last night?'

'No—go away!' Hare cried. 'Desmond at Rix's?'

'Yes, rather! I simply walked out without seeing the fellow.'

'Really? By Jove!'

'Yes; and Pat just grinned as if Desmond was an old pal of his.'

Hare laughed. 'Perhaps he is.'

Gregory laughed too, though he couldn't see any joke about O'Shane's annoying behaviour. 'I tried to get at Rix about it, and he said that if I wasn't interested enough to stay when Desmond was there he couldn't be bothered retailing the conversation. But this morning someone mentioned Desmond, and Allerick said, "Hang Desmond!" and glared fit to kill.'

'No wonder, after the mess Leigh's made of the museum,' said Hare. 'Oh well, it was soon straightened up. Someone had a sense of humour.'

'Sense of humour? Really, Hare, I can't understand you sometimes.'

'How unfortunate,' smiled Hare, and meant exactly the opposite. As Gregory and Robson strolled away, he noticed O'Shane coming out of the door. 'Pat!' he called.

O'Shane swung round. ''Lo, Whiskers. What's up?' He started to walk back to meet Hare, when, to his astonishment, he was intercepted by Desmond.

'O'Shane, can I have a word with you?' said the captain of Leigh's.

'Two, old son,' said O'Shane cheerily, as though no such things as separate Houses existed.

'Come round to my den after second

lesson, then,' went on Desmond. 'And, I
say, don't mention it to anyone, will you?
I'd come round to your study, only . . .
Well, will you?'

'Certainly, Desmond; like a shot! So
long. Don't mind me mentioning—will you?
—but your jolly old lip's beginning to look
gory again.'

Desmond pulled out his handkerchief hastily
as Hare came up. He did not know exactly
what Hare's feelings towards him were, so,
rather than sound them, he walked quickly
away.

'I don't think Rix would be pleased if he
saw you jawing to Desmond,' Hare murmured,
as they walked across the quadrangle.

'I don't mind annoying old Rix once in
a while. What do you think of Desmond,
Whiskers?'

'He seems a decent chap. He's good-
looking.'

'But his character?'

'I never judge anyone,' Hare remarked
definitely.

'Silly ass!' smiled O'Shane. 'Well, I'll
tell you what I think—Desmond's one of
the best chaps going.'

'You say that about everyone. Rix
wouldn't be pleased.'

'You've got Rix on the brain. Why keep chucking him at my head?'

'It seems the correct thing to start shouting about Rix whenever anyone mentions Desmond, that's all.'

'Blow Rix!'

'Sh-sh!' exclaimed Hare in mock horror. 'Walls have ears.'

As though in answer to their thoughts, Allerick himself appeared round the corner. 'I say, you chaps,' were his very first words, 'what about getting up a rag to pay Leigh's out for mucking up the museum?'

'Need we bother?' asked Hare quietly.

Allerick's glance seemed to wither the very grass. 'Need we! Are you going to let an insult like that pass?'

'We got it straightened up in time!' O'Shane ventured to put in.

'They didn't intend us to. Look here, you two, are you going over to Leigh's?'

'No; don't be daft,' said O'Shane.

'We couldn't,' added Hare without enthusiasm.

'Then what shall we do?'

'Get some of the rest of the chaps to work,' suggested Hare. 'Our brains are tired.'

Allerick gave an incoherent growl and went away.

'One can't help making comparisons, some-times,' O'Shane said very, very quietly.

'No, that's true,' answered Hare. And added a moment later, as though it had no connection, 'Desmond is such a cheerful old horse.'

CHAPTER IV.

THEFT !

THE library of St Martin's was a beautiful room. It ran the full length of the front of the School, on the second storey, and had three wide bay-windows overlooking the quadrangle, the School lane, and the village with its lane down to the yellow shore, and, last of all, the stretch of cool green sea fading into the purple sky. Inside, these windows were provided with comfortable seats where fellows could sit and jaw at will, or merely watch the doings of the people in the quadrangle below, or the ships passing on the sea beyond. On the other side of the room there were two doors, one at each end of the hall-balcony. Through one of these now, on this shining June afternoon, the School had begun to file. Loring came first, then two or three prefects, and then the School House part of the Fifth. After each group of boys came a prefect to keep order. They marched

At last Allerick came, more sullen and awkward than usual, and the cloud lifted from his face a little as he gazed at the shining display. He turned eagerly round to speak to the one who followed him, and found himself looking into the blue eyes of Desmond, already leading in his House. With a bitten-off exclamation of disgust he swung round again, clumsily knocking against the table.

'Careful, careful!' said the Head-master. Allerick turned crimson, and walked the length of the table, scarcely looking at it again. But Desmond was all eagerness. He was so long standing there that D'Arcy gave him a little push, for the chaps behind were getting impatient; then he appeared to wake out of a day-dream, and strode on smiling.

'Thank you very much, sir,' said O'Shane, as Lord Inverslowe finished his story.

'But if you're Irish,' Lord Inverslowe said, appearing to like O'Shane very much, 'I know what will interest you. This Necra medallion——' He moved towards the centre of the table, and stretched his hand to take the plush case. For a moment his fat fingers hovered there, then he drew in his breath a little sharply, and said impatiently, 'Please pass the medallion whoever has it.'

There were five or six boys round the table then, the last of Leigh's House, including McLaren, Waugh, and Sikes. They looked up when Lord Inverslowe spoke, but none of them had anything in their hands.

Lord Inverslowe frowned a little, and turned to Dr Newton. 'Did you move the medallion, Tony?' he asked, and McLaren gave an audible grunt at the nickname.

But the Head did not seem to notice Lord Inverslowe's unwary use of it in the presence of the boys. 'No, I haven't got it,' he answered. 'Do you mean to say it's not——' He leaned over to look in the case. Sure enough the medallion was gone. The Head's face whitened a little, but he would not admit the presence of the awful thought which had entered his brain. He lifted the case and held it up. 'One moment!' he said.

The boys who were just about to pass out, Lestrange and Telford, turned at the words. The others remained at the table.

'If you remember, boys,' the Head-master said, 'I asked you to obtain permission before examining the curios. Whoever has the Necra medallion, please pass it back.'

There was no answer. McLaren stooped to look on the floor and under the table, thinking perhaps the precious thing had fallen there. But no, it had not.

For fully two minutes they all stood there as though carved in stone. Lord Inverslowe looked exceedingly worried, but his worry was nothing to Dr Newton's. The Headmaster seemed to become older and harder. A moment ago he had appeared happy and proud, almost boyish. Very sternly he said at last, 'Please close both doors.'

Lestrange hastened to obey. 'Boys,' said Dr Newton, 'you know as well as I do what the removal of the medallion might be called.' He appeared to have great difficulty in speaking so before Lord Inverslowe, old school-friend though the latter was. 'The honour of the School is at stake. If this is a joke, it is a foolish and even a wicked one. The medallion was here a few minutes ago—I was admiring its beauty. I looked away again—it has gone. You see, I did not think it was necessary to watch, policeman-like, the doings of this School.' He looked round at the eight boys in the room. Lestrange still stood by the door, looking down at the floor. McLaren had drawn his shoulders up, his ugly face

was set in an intense and forbidding frown.
Waugh's red face was redder than usual,
Horton merely looked angry, and fidgeted.
The other four, who were Fifth-form boys,
stood together at the end of the table, very
nervous and surprised.

When the Head stopped speaking, Lestrange
spoke. 'The case was empty when I came to
the table, sir,' he said. 'I noticed it, but I
thought Lord Inverslowe was showing the—
the—contents to O'Shane, sir.'

'I did not notice any medallion, sir,' Waugh
said. And the other two chimed in with,
'Nor I, sir.'

'The medallion was most noticeable,' the
Head answered; 'it was the most striking
and valuable thing in the whole collection.—
Did you see it, boys?' he asked the four
Fifth-formers. They denied any knowledge
of it.

'Then it must have been removed before
you entered the room, Lestrange,' the Head
went on. 'Oh, this is terrible! Terrible!'

'Now, Tony, don't get upset,' said Lord
Inverslowe kindly, putting his hand on
Dr Newton's shoulder. 'Boys will be boys.'

'But not thieves,' the Head said.

'Oh, it's only a joke!' Lord Inverslowe
even endeavoured to smile.

'No, it's not a joke,' the Head answered grimly. 'Waugh, ring the bell for the whole School to assemble in the hall.'

'Yes, sir.' Waugh went, and very glad he was to go, too.

'You others may go. It is presumed for the present that the medallion was gone before you entered the room.'

The boys went, and the Head-master turned to Lord Inverslowe. 'I 'll help you to fix these things up again, Harry. The medallion may possibly have got hidden by one of them.' In silence they started to pack the treasures up again. They were both at a loss for words.

'The boys will be in hall by now,' Dr Newton said at last almost curtly. 'Will you come, Inverslowe, or will you trust me to carry the business through?'

'Do whatever you can, Tony,' his friend said. 'I 'm sorry this has occurred—more sorry than I can say. It 's as much my fault as anyone's. I should have arranged the collection with more care.'

'The School has always been worthy of trust up to now,' the Head answered. 'Nothing like this has occurred before. Well, I will go and conduct a thorough examination of the whole School.' He went out, leaving Lord Inverslowe wrapping up the last of the treasures.

In the hall below, the School was congregated, the news had spread over the two hundred boys, there was a hum of low whispering, which died as they saw the Head pacing solemnly along the balcony. He looked down over the crowd of them. What fine young fellows they were—so erect, so straight and clear-eyed. And now it seemed that one of them was a thief. 'Well, live and learn,' thought the Head, as he walked down the stairs, the centre of all those eyes. 'Live and learn.' He mounted the dais. Now there was dead silence. For a moment he wondered how to begin. Should he distrust them all and demand a search of everyone? No, the thing could perhaps be done better than that.

'Boys,' he began very calmly, 'you know what has happened. As yet I am not going to explain how terrible it is. Perhaps there is one boy here who would like to have again the last half-hour, that he might act differently. That is impossible. We all act on impulse and make mistakes. But this one boy, to whom alone I am now speaking, shall have the equivalent of that half-hour. He shall have five minutes in which to undo

the wrong he has done. He has but to walk
across into my study and no more. He has
five minutes in which to brace himself for
atonement, and no more.'

So he said, and the silence descended again.
It was the longest five minutes St Martin's
had ever known. They heard Lord Inverslowe walk to the door of the library, as
though he were going out on to the balcony,
then he stopped, changed his mind and went
back. They heard, far away, a man in the
School lane playing 'Rock of Ages' on a
whistle. They heard someone opening and
closing the door of the masters' common-
room. But what they did not hear was the
slow foot-fall of a boy moving towards the
Head's study. They waited till the five
minutes were over, but it did not come.

'Very well, then,' said the Head, a new
note in his voice. 'Who was the boy who
asked the question about the Necra medallion?
I think it related to its value.'

'It was I, sir,' Crewe answered immediately,
and though he was a boy who would not have
stolen a pen-nib, he went as red as a poppy.

'Yes, Crewe, you may go. The medallion
was certainly there when you left the table.
Now, one boy examined it. Wendell, I
think, was it not?'

' Yes, sir,' Wendell answered. ' I lifted it out of the case.'

' And returned it. I saw it then myself. You came last of the School House line, did you not ? '

' Yes, sir.'

' Very well. School House, dismiss ! '

The School House marched away, obviously disappointed at missing the rest of the affair.

' Allerick ! ' called the Head.

Allerick started violently, and stumbling over somebody's foot, walked clumsily up to the platform. ' Yes, sir.'

' In what order did Wright's House file through ? '

' O'Shane went first, sir,' he answered. ' Then the Fifth form, with King and Spencer; then the Fourth, with Gregory and Cairns, I think——'

' Is that right ? ' the Head broke in. ' Did you two boys take charge of the Fourth form ? '

' Yes, sir,' answered Gregory and King in duet.

' Well, Allerick ? '

' Then the Third form came, sir ; then Hare and Robson ; then I followed Robson. I was the last.'

' I see. And then ? '

Desmond led Leigh's House in,' said Allerick, for no apparent reason going violently red.

'Well, that will do, Allerick,' said the Head after a moment's thought. 'Desmond!' He knew it was wrong to let such a change come into his voice, but he could hardly help it. Desmond strode forward, his fine head lifted proudly, his eyes very dark and blue. Dr Newton spoke very coldly to him, for he hated favouritism. 'Desmond, was the medallion in its case when you reached the table ?'

'Would you mind describing it to me, sir ? I seemed to get a general idea of the collection rather than notice any particular thing.'

'You would have noticed the Necra medallion,' Dr Newton answered. 'It was about the size of a penny, red-gold, carved with the figure of a woman with long hair, and wreathed with roses. Round the edge were sixty dark rubies, each set deep into the solid gold.'

'Then it was not there,' answered Desmond with certainty.

'Are you sure, Desmond ?'

'Yes, sir. There was nothing answering to that description on the table.'

The Head paused. 'Thank you, Desmond,'

he said at last; it never entering his mind
not to take Desmond's word, even in a matter
like this. 'We will go back again, then,' the
Head went on. 'But first, seeing they can
have nothing to do with it, Leigh's House
may go. I am afraid this rests with Wright's.'

For a moment Allerick turned and looked
at Desmond. If ever sheer hate looked out
of anyone's eyes, it looked out of Allerick's
then. Very ugly and very angry he looked,
and Desmond's own eyes clouded as he met
the glance, and he glared back. But when
Allerick had turned again, he was sorry he
had done it, and sorry for Allerick. For it
must be rotten to be captain of a House in
which, possibly, there is a low-down thief.
Desmond could imagine the stinging shame
he would have felt if the Head's words had
been: 'I am afraid this rests with Leigh's.'
Poor old Allerick.

But there was more to come. He turned
Leigh's out, but the Head said, 'Afterwards,
Desmond, come back—and please bring Loring.
The captains of the three Houses must be
here.'

'Yes, sir,' answered Desmond, and felt even
sorrier for Allerick.

'Now,' the Head continued, 'let me see.'
He cast his glance over the lines of boys,

and noticed Hare, still standing at the back of the Third-form line. 'Hare!' he called.

Hare marched up to the platform. He was self-conscious and his cheeks burned, but his steady grey eyes met the Head's with absolute fearlessness.

'Was the medallion there when you left the table, Hare?'

Everyone noticed, and no one more than Hare himself, that the Head-master had begun to say 'left the table' instead of 'reached the table,' as he had done hitherto.

'Yes, sir,' answered Hare.

The Head searched the boy's face for a moment, then he said, without questioning Hare further, 'You may go, Hare.—Every boy who entered the library before Hare may go, too.'

A few minutes later Desmond returned with Loring, to find that the Head had descended from the platform, and instead of all Wright's House, there were now only Robson and Allerick. Robson was cool and almost unconcerned, but Allerick was going red and white every second.

'We have got so far, Loring,' the Head said, as the two drew near; 'the medallion was there when Hare went, and gone when Desmond reached the table. Of course, we

may get to a point when no one's word can
be taken, but perhaps we may reach a conclusion before then.'

Desmond and Loring were dumbfounded.
So the Head meant that either Robson or
Allerick was a thief?

'Robson,' said Dr Newton, 'did you see
the medallion?'

'Yes, sir.' Robson was perfectly calm, he
did not appear to have grasped the fact that
he was under suspicion.

'You are sure it was in its case, on the
centre of the table?'

'Quite undisturbed, sir. I noticed it particularly. In fact, I hardly looked at anything else on the table.'

'Thank you, Robson. But you had better
remain. Mind, I am not doubting your word,
any more than I doubted Hare's, but the
thing seems to have narrowed down.'

Desmond thought then that if such a great
man as the Head *could* make a mistake, he
was making it now. Allerick looked positively
murderous.

'Allerick,' said the Head, 'what was your
impression of that table?'

'I—I——' Allerick stuttered, obviously too
indignant to be coherent.

Desmond remembered how Allerick had

turned round, then in his disgust had banged into the table, causing everything on it to rattle. He broke into Allerick's stammering speech. 'He turned round, sir——'

'Desmond!' snapped the Head; 'I addressed Allerick, not you. Please reserve your comments until they are invited.'

Desmond flushed to the roots of his hair— a hot painful red.

As though he had taken heart from his enemy's discomfort, Allerick found his voice. 'I didn't notice anything at all on the table, sir. I was thinking of something else.'

'Do you mean to say you did not look at the collection?'

'I *looked*, sir; but I—I——' He could not explain. Desmond alone knew what he could have said.

'Was the medallion there then?' the Head flung at him sternly.

'I don't know,' was all Allerick could answer.

'Do you realise what this means, Allerick?'

Allerick was overcome by a violent fit of temper. 'You trusted Robson,' he broke out, almost forgetting he spoke to the Head-master; 'and you trusted Desmond; but because I didn't notice the collection, you think I'm the thief! Why should you believe Desmond any more than me?' he went on, losing all respect. 'Desmond wasn't sure whether the medallion was gone or not. Desmond——' He realised that he was blazoning his hatred of Desmond for them all to see, and stopped suddenly.

The Head's expression had not changed, but his voice was very cold as he said, 'You must restrain yourself, Allerick. This affair is a strain to the nerves of us all, but it must be faced without flinching. I have no intention of distrusting you. Do you know anything of the disappearance of the Necra medallion?'

'Of course not,' Allerick retorted, but with less heat.

'You forget yourself. You mean "No, sir." Do you know anything about the loss of the medallion, Allerick?'

'No, sir,' Allerick answered quietly, but sullenly.

'If you care to search me, I am quite prepared,' said Desmond calmly.

'No, no——' Dr Newton began, then stopped. 'Come into this room,' he ordered, remembering he was responsible to Lord Inverslowe for the return of the medallion.

Loring searched the three. Desmond helped him to search his own person, in a half-smiling fashion. Robson seemed a little annoyed at such an undignified procedure, and straightened his tie in a finicky fashion when Loring had finished with him. But Allerick was angry and sullen, he made jerky movements of resentment, and looked murderously at Desmond for suggesting the search. But the medallion was not on any of them, unless the thief had some ingenious method of concealing it.

The Head was relieved, but he smiled wearily. 'We're no further. I couldn't doubt any of you,' he said. 'Oh, I wish . . . Thank you, you may all go.' As they moved hazily away, he sat down on the edge of the dais.

Desmond, last to go, turned round and moved a few steps back, preparing to speak.

The Head looked up and half-frowned. 'Did you hear, Desmond ? You may go !'

'Yes, sir,' said Desmond, and went—his face very pale.

The Head-master looked after him and smiled ruefully. He ran his fingers through his black hair, and the action made him look suddenly as young as the captain of Leigh's himself.

CHAPTER V.

ALLERICK.

THE captain of Wright's walked back to his study with thunder in his eyes and a bent head. Hare passed him in the hall-passage and tried to speak, but Allerick passed as though he had seen no one, and entering his study, drew the door to with a loud bang. Arrived there, he behaved strangely. He strode most purposefully over to the grate and kicked at the glowing coals with all his might, damaging his shoe considerably and causing clouds of smoke to rise. There were some books on the table, quite a pile of them. He threw one on the desk, one on the chair, and the rest he merely swept on to the floor, then he drew a chair up to the table and sat down, resting his head on his shaking hands.

A minute or two passed, then the door opened and Pindlethwaite, small, untidy, and impudent, entered. 'Shall I get tea?' he inquired.

'No. Get out!' growled Allerick.

'Where do you get "out" from?' asked Piffle, thinking that such a capital joke that he commenced to gurgle like an overfilled kettle. He approached the table. 'Eh, Allerick?' he persisted.

Allerick's arm shot, and he smacked the side of the little boy's head.

'Yah!' said Piffle, considerably taken aback, and hastily moving towards the door. 'Bear! Cock-eyed snake!' he yelled. 'Fat whale, yellow-eyed gorilla, mat-hair——' Then his powers of invention running out, he continued, 'Bully, coward, brute!'

The beautiful epithets had no effect on Allerick, who remained glaring ahead of him, too deep in his thoughts to bother getting up.

'Cad,' continued Piffle, waxing bolder as Allerick did not move. 'Thief!'

'What?' In one bound Allerick was upon the little boy, dragging him against the table by his coat-collar. 'What? How dare you? You . . . I'll teach you! . . . I'll . . .' He shook the poor Piffle as a terrier shakes a rat.

Pindlethwaite was alarmed, and when Allerick's grip hurt, digging into his flesh, he began to whimper like some small animal. Allerick gave a snarl, and pushed him roughly aside. He did not intend to be cruel, but Pindlethwaite overbalanced and fell against the table-leg.

'What on earth's the matter?' came O'Shane's voice suddenly from the doorway. He stared at Allerick in amazement, and striding towards Piffle, put the child on his feet again.

'He hit me—he knocked me down—he choked me—he throttled me,' Piffle recited in shrill tones, retreating behind his saviour and locking his small arms round the Irishman's slim form. 'Don't let him touch me, I didn't do anything—I didn't.'

'What's up?' O'Shane asked, staring at Allerick as though he thought his friend had taken leave of his senses. He looked in amazement at the books lying on the floor and the scattered coals on the hearth.

Allerick suddenly thrust his hands into his pockets and sank wearily into the easy-chair again.

'You'd better go, Piffle,' O'Shane said. 'I'll get tea.'

Piffle did not need a second telling. He gave a whoop of joy and, all his troubles forgotten, disappeared down the passage like a flash.

O'Shane quietly closed the door and, without speaking, picked up and tidied the books, put the cloth on the table, and started to get out the cups and saucers.

Allerick looked up as O'Shane put the kettle on the fire, raking the ashes away in a business-like fashion. 'I don't want any tea, Pat,' he growled ungraciously.

'Och, you're going to have some!' answered O'Shane sweetly, and went blithely on with his preparations. Presently he commenced to whistle, 'The more we are together.'

'For goodness' sake, shut up!' snapped Allerick.

'I'll go as soon as we've had tea,' O'Shane said; 'so long as I'm in the way.'

'I'm not hinting at you to go,' Allerick growled.

'Well, I won't then, old man,' O'Shane said in the tone of one receiving a great favour.

'What do you think of it all?' Allerick burst out, when at last they were sitting at the table. In spite of his saying he wanted no tea, Allerick was making a good job of it, eating hurriedly as though he scarcely knew what he was doing.

'All what?'

'You know jolly well, you ass. All this medallion business. Do you know the Head as good as accused me of pinching the rotten thing?'

'Go on!' O'Shane looked up from his cold sausage with startled eyes.

Allerick duly explained the process of detection.

O'Shane grinned. 'That's not accusing you. That's just messing,' he answered elegantly. 'I wouldn't give it a second thought.'

'You would if it was you who were left odd man out kind o' thing,' Allerick told him; but, nevertheless, he looked decidedly more cheerful.

'The Head shouldn't have done such a thing,' O'Shane went on. 'But I dare say he saw his mistake as well as anyone. Who came before you, did you say—Whiskers?'

'No—Robbie.'

'And Desmond after you?'

'Yes.'

'Well, either of them are as likely to have pinched it as you, and the Newt knows jolly well. I dare say Desmond just didn't notice it.'

Allerick looked up, and was about to speak; then he closed his lips tightly, as though to bite the words back.

'The thing'll have to be done properly,'

O'Shane said firmly; 'on proper lines. The thief must be gone for as he tries to palm it off. I say, Rix, I wonder who *did* take it?'

'I did, of course,' Allerick answered. '·The Head's got Desmond's word for it, hasn't he?' His tone was the acme of bitterness.

O'Shane frowned. 'See here, Rix, there's no use being nasty,' he said; 'Desmond's got nothing to do with it.'

'Hang Desmond!' Allerick exclaimed.

'He's one of the best chaps going,' O'Shane said hotly.

'Is that what you gained from your morning's interview with him?'

'How on earth . . . Who told you I was jawing to Des this morning?'

'You were, weren't you? Peace and good-will, I suppose. Desmond's friendly overtures have a way of turning out nastily.'

'I don't know what you're talking about,' O'Shane answered steadily. 'You're in a vile temper, anyway. You couldn't be more depressed if you *had* stolen the jewel.'

'Oh, shut up, shut up!' Allerick exclaimed. 'Go and hang round Desmond!'

'He's certainly more gracious,' O'Shane smiled, rising and beginning to clear away the tea-things. 'But it's a good thing I'm a good-natured fellow, Rix, I must say.'

'Where's your trumpeter?' Allerick rolled up the lid of his desk, and pulled out his exercise-books.

O'Shane laughed and commenced to change into gym-shoes. 'I'm going to have a go at the parallel-bars, Rix,' he said. 'Are you coming, or are you going to work?'

'Neither. I'm going to write a letter.'

'To Eileen? I see. So long. I hope it improves your temper. Ta-ta.' He went out, smiling cheerily.

Allerick, his shoulders hunched in an ugly fashion, stared dully at the note-paper. He did not attempt to write. Before him there hung steadily a vision of a handsome face, flushed, and out of its bright fairness shone a pair of vivid sea-blue eyes—Desmond of Leigh's.

There was a knock at the door.

'Come in!' Allerick said impatiently, and swung round. In the doorway the vision which had haunted him materialised—Desmond stood there, straight and tall. Allerick, stung by the thought of his own short sallowness, thought that Desmond did not fit the brilliant green and blue blazer, the spruce white-flannel trousers. He should have been wearing a skin jacket, a golden helmet, a sword; his hair should be unchecked, hanging in a shining riot about his broad shoulders. How he hated him!

'Well?' growled Allerick.

Desmond strode forward eagerly. It was something at least to be admitted to the study of the captain of Wright's.

'I want to say . . . about this medallion affair, you know . . .' Desmond was never very good at introducing a subject of conversation, and now he realised that he was very clumsy indeed.

Allerick stood up—his temper, not very well in hand, rising again. 'I've heard enough about the thing,' he said. 'Why don't you tell the whole School I stole it? I don't care——'

'Oh listen, Allerick! I say, do keep your wool on,' Desmond got in eagerly. 'We ought to pull together . . . I mean . . .' for Allerick was glaring fiercely now.

'I think you said something about "pulling together" last night, didn't you? And I think we "pulled together" this morning, didn't we? Get out, Desmond——'

'But—Allerick, you don't see——'

'I see that if you don't go, I'll throw you out!'

'Oh, I'll go!' Desmond crossed to the door. 'But I wish you'd listen, for the

School's sake. Perhaps when you've cooled down——'

'Do you want the rest of your teeth loosened?' Allerick asked, clenching his fists.

'No, thank you.' Desmond was perfectly calm, because he was so sorry for Allerick. 'Good-night.' He went, leaving the door open.

Presently Allerick rose, intending to shut the door, but was prevented by the entrance of Hare. 'Hang it, when *am* I going to get a chance to write? What do you want, Whiskers?' he demanded.

'I just wanted to know what happened after I left the hall, Rix. It was such a funny thing for the Head to do. I couldn't understand his method. It really looked as if——'

'I'd pinched it. Yes, it did,' Allerick growled.

'But Robson——'

'Oh, Robbie saw the beastly thing, and I didn't. I'm the thief all right, just because I didn't happen to notice whether the thing was there or not.'

Hare stared in astonishment hearing the angry voice. 'I say, Rix, you're taking it to heart, aren't you? Why worry?'

'You're as bad as Pat,' Allerick answered.

'Would you worry if you were accused of theft?'

'Not if I hadn't done it,' said Hare. His voice was cold, he looked Allerick directly across the eyes.

'So you think I *did* steal it?'

'I think you're very foolish being rude to your friends, Rix. Especially just at present. I know as little as you do about the affair. Probably Desmond was mistaken in thinking the medallion was there. But I wouldn't speak as if he said it wasn't there just for the purpose of casting suspicion on *you*. Why, this might be the saving of both the Houses. If they pull together——'

The two words acted on Allerick as a red rag to a bull. He rose, almost knocking his chair over. 'See here, Whiskers, cut out the preaching,' he yelled. 'I've had enough. When I've pinched a few more medallions you can begin to reform me, but not till then.'

Hare smiled. 'Come for a stroll round the field, Rix,' he suggested; 'mugging in here's frayed your temper.'

For answer Allerick turned round again, pulling the note-paper towards him. So Hare went, as O'Shane and Desmond before him had done, wondering at Allerick's evil temper.

And none of the three guessed that the medallion had little or nothing to do with it.

Allerick began to write again, at first with many pauses, but at last he lost himself in the letter, and his hot colour began to fade; he grew calmer. He finished the letter and glanced up at the clock. It was a quarter past eight. He had just time to get down into the village for a stamp and to post the letter before call-over; and he would miss any further visitors with sympathy and good advice. He thrust the letter into his blazer pocket and went out. The sun was just setting, and a rather blinding yellow light hung over the place. White figures moved on the playing-fields, and occasionally a voice cried praise or blame. Allerick strode along the narrow lane; he was facing the sea now, and the cool wind was refreshing. He would catch the post, and the letter would reach its destination next day. He never on any account allowed Piffle to take his letters to Eileen to the post, because he did not want it spread over the whole School that the captain of Wright's wrote to a girl. He could imagine the jokes that would fly around. 'She must be blind'; or, 'Oh well, there's no accounting for some people's taste!' or, 'Beauty and the Beast,' and so on. Allerick smiled at the thought. There was no one whose good opinion he cared so much for except the Head's and . . . No, he hated Desmond. How could he care what he thought? Oh, hang the fellow! Why couldn't he think of something else?

He arrived at the post-office, and was about to go in, when he noticed a little collarette in the window of the shop next door. It was a funny little old jumble of a shop, where curios were sold, old prints, pottery, and quaint jewellery. The owner of the shop was a little old man like a withered apple, and he was interested in anything that was strange or beautiful. He bought old pottery and jewellery of all descriptions, not always to sell again, but because he loved it, and seemed to have an endless supply of money. It was rumoured that there was wealth untold behind that little narrow shop with its stout iron-edged shutters.

Allerick went up to the window and studied the collarette. It was of pale cream lace, and had a design of roses and leaves. It was only five shillings, and Eileen would love it. He decided to buy it and put it in the letter. He could get a new envelope at the post-office, and address it there. He felt in his pocket to make sure that he had enough loose cash, and then entered the shop.

As soon as he did so he saw Sikes, who was looking at a tray of varnished butter-flies—another strange commodity in which old Mr Dowling dealt.

Allerick turned to go out again, he wasn't going to let that little Leigh's worm see him buy a girl's collarette. But Sikes had turned round and seen him, so Allerick went boldly up to the counter. Sikes bent over the tray, pretending not to notice him.

'Well, young gentleman,' old Dowling mumbled, his creased face becoming more seamed than ever, 'what can I do for you this fine evening?'

'I'll wait until you've finished with your other customer,' Allerick answered.

Sikes looked up in surprise, and stared at Allerick without smiling.

'Oh well, well—right, right,' murmured Dowling. 'Private business. Doesn't do to tell a crowd. No, no. I know—I see— I understand.'

Sikes selected a butterfly, his vacillating mind made up for the present. As soon as he left the shop he would regret his choice,

but he had been here nearly twenty minutes,
and it would be call-over soon. ' I 'll have
this one,' he said. 'Thank you. Good-night.'
He walked very slowly to the door, but
Allerick was waiting until he had gone
before speaking to Mr Dowling.

Sikes left the shop, and opening the little
case in his hand, looked at the beautiful
Brazilian moth within. Immediately he
wished he had bought the pale blue butterfly that had such perfect edges to its wings.
He almost turned to go back, then he
thought perhaps he would be kept another
twenty minutes. Besides, Allerick would
think he was trying to spy on him. As if
he cared what Allerick was going to buy!
Nevertheless, the first words he said to
Horton when he entered their study were:
' I say, Hor, who do you think was in
Dowling's? Allerick.'

' Well?' Horton looked up from the
Cricket Times impatiently.

' And he wouldn't tell Dowling what he
wanted until I 'd gone. Said he 'd wait
until the other customer was finished with.'

' What? At Dowling's? I say . . .'
Horton began to be interested; he was an
incorrigible gossip, and anything about the
hated Wright's House interested him. ' Isn't

Dowling's the place where they buy old
jewellery stuff?'

'Yes; anything in that line.'

Horton fell into silence for a moment,
then he said, with apparent carelessness,
'By the way, Allerick's a queer stick—isn't
he?'

'Yes, Hor. Did you hear what Waugh
said about the Head's thinning the medallion business down to him? I don't know
whether it's only a rumour, but——'

'Oh, it's true enough! But it was only
a casual process,' Horton said, with a faint
regret in his tones. 'I believe Allerick
resented it awfully. He's a mighty queer
stick.'

'Yes, Hor,' agreed Sikes again meekly,
and with absolute insincerity.

'Looks jolly fishy,' Horton murmured,
and commenced to whistle softly.

CHAPTER VI.

THE STRENGTH OF SUSPICION.

A WEEK passed, and St Martin's was no nearer to a solution of the missing medallion. Dr Newton lay awake at night trying to discover a way in which it could have been stolen. He remembered Allerick's clumsy manner as he passed the table, and his anger at being questioned. But surely it was impossible that Allerick should steal. But three facts, well known to the School, haunted the Head. In the first place, Allerick was poor, and had been trying without success to gain a scholarship for Cambridge, and his failure was hitting him hard. In the second place, he called himself a Communist, and had given lectures which had been a source of great amusement and derision in Wright's common-room. In these lectures, though frequently interrupted, he had preached the equality of man, and insisted that wealth should not belong only to certain members of the race. In the third place, Allerick knew a lot about the treasures found by

excavation, and had written essays on the
subject for the School magazine. ' Oh,
coincidence, coincidence!' cried the Head-
master to himself; yet he knew Allerick was
getting more unpopular with his House day
by day, and the feud between Leigh's and
Wright's was gathering strength in spite of
all Desmond's manly efforts to check it.

Besides all this, Lord Inverslowe was beginning to get exceedingly worried about the
Necra medallion, and although he had turned
down Dr Newton's suggestion—made with
great bravery—to put the matter in the
hands of the police, the Head-master knew
that it was only for his sake he did so, and
that if the medallion was not found, the
police would have to come into the affair
eventually.

Another person who took the matter to
heart was Desmond. He noticed how the
discussion of the theft seemed to bring the
worst out of everyone, and, as he said to
D'Arcy, he wished from the bottom of his
heart the beastly thing would turn up.
' Every chap looks askance at everyone else,'
he said angrily one evening. ' I begin actually
to feel guilty myself when they say: " Are
you *sure* the medallion was gone when you
reached the table?" I go red.'

'Yes, you do, son,' agreed D'Arcy, with a broad grin. 'But then, you go red if a fly looks at you,' he added.

'I've never noticed any flies looking at me,' Desmond murmured; 'but I suppose you know all about their taste. But what I was going to say was how I hate all this business of hinting, and so on.'

'What do you mean, Des?' D'Arcy asked. Nothing troubled D'Arcy much, but he was quick to notice if Desmond was upset. And Desmond was. He had been half-hearted at his cricket-practice; he had taken no joy in being captain of Leigh's; he had lost half his happy conceit.

'I mean the way chaps go on about old Rix. If he sneezes, they say it's his guilty conscience. Two or three of those pigs over at Wright's have made up their minds that he stole the medallion, and they're spreading their beastly suspicions as rapidly as they can.'

'It's not only Wright's,' D'Arcy answered; 'it's here as well.'

'That's beastly unsporting,' Desmond said angrily, the colour rushing into his cheeks. 'Who's got any right to say anything, whatever House they belong to? There isn't even circumstantial evidence against Allerick.'

'I say, old man, you're mighty fond of old Rix all of a sudden, aren't you?' asked D'Arcy. 'Have your teeth hardened again yet?'

'Don't fool,' replied Desmond sweetly. 'I'm serious. It's not that I care so much for old Rix, but I'd think it rotten to say things about anyone the way they do. But what the Aunt Kate do you mean by saying Leigh's are doing it too? Do you mean just because Allerick belongs to Wright's?' If that's it, it's perfectly rotten, and I'll knock down anyone who says anything to me.'

'It's nothing much,' D'Arcy said. 'I think Horton originated it. Horton's hot against Wright's; he carries things a bit too far.'

'He does that,' Desmond agreed emphatically, for he disliked Horton. 'Go on, Darkie.'

'About last week, Horton said Allerick went into Dowling's when Sikes was there, and wouldn't say what he wanted until Dowling and he were alone.' D'Arcy tried to speak nonchalantly, to hide the fact that Horton's news had affected him.

Desmond gave him a quick glance. 'What rot! Dowling's, the jewellers?'

'Yes.'

'So they make out that—that——'

D'Arcy finished the sentence for him. 'That poor old Rix was trying to make Dowling fork out a substantial sum for the Necra medallion. They say that Rix will probably be rolling. Poor old Rix—and the beggar's so hard up.'

'He is that. I believe he won't be able to go to Cambridge if he doesn't get a schol. It makes things all the more rotten for him.'

'As I think I observed before, anyone would think Rix was your long-lost son,' D'Arcy teased him.

'Stop rotting,' Desmond commanded. 'Why, the chap hates me! But it is rotten. I know he could barely stump up half a crown for that hospital sub a few weeks ago. I think some chaps are awful rotters.'

Telford burst in upon them without knocking. 'I say, you two, the Newt's asked me to collect for the new wing at Ranley Hospital. Here's the list.' He tossed a slightly crumpled sheet of paper on to the table.

Desmond picked it up. 'I'll give thirty bob,' he said. 'Darkie and I were just saying . . .' He broke off, and went very red, staring at the list.

'What's up?' inquired the Tiger.

'Look here, Darkie, that's rather funny—er—considering, isn't it?' Desmond said, a slight catch of amazement in his voice.

D'Arcy took the paper. The beginning of the list read:

Dr A. J. Newton . . £10	0	0
Rev. M. Saunders . . 2	2	0
S. Loring 1	0	0
B. D. Allerick . . . 5	0	0

D'Arcy laughed rather too loudly, and said, 'Old Rix was pretty generous, wasn't he?'

'Oh—Allerick!' smiled the Tiger, who had not heard the latest tale about the captain of Wright's. 'Yes. Looks as if he'd come into a fortune or something, doesn't it?'

'Why?' asked Desmond fiercely.

'Don't bite me!' the Tiger exclaimed. 'Why the ferocious look? I mean—Rix could never rise higher than five bob for anything else.'

'I say, Des, wouldn't it be awful if he'd put the five in the wrong column, and could only afford a bare crown?'

'Nothin' doin', Darkie,' laughed the Tiger. 'He's stumped up, cash down. Anyway, why are you so frightfully interested in Allerick's sub?'

'Oh, tell him the rotten tale, Darkie,' ordered Desmond; 'he evidently hasn't heard it yet.'

D'Arcy recounted the episode at Dowling's.

Telford did not seem impressed. 'It's probably only a yarn,' he commented. 'It's like one of Horton's rotten tales. Horton'd say Wright's were toads with giraffe tails if he thought anyone'd believe him. And there's definitely a weak spot in this particular yarn.'

'Oh—where?' asked Desmond eagerly.

'Well, if it was queer for Rix to be in Dowling's, why was Sikes there? Dowling's is open to the general public, isn't it?'

'But, you ass,' Desmond put in, 'the point is, Rix wouldn't say what he wanted to buy or sell.'

'Anyway, Sikes was supposed to be getting moths or something.'

'Just what he would get,' the Tiger announced. 'He's moth-eaten. And Horton's got Wright's on the brain. Anyway, I wouldn't believe Allerick had stolen it unless I had infallible proof, which doesn't seem to be forthcoming—and don't think it will be. Rix steal! Not likely!'

'It does one good to hear you, Tiger,' said Desmond warmly. 'I think the affair should be tackled properly. If fellows are going to say the medallion was taken to Dowling's, Dowling's ought to be examined. But this underhand chummering gets on my nerves.'

'Your nerves?' D'Arcy chuckled. 'Where do you keep them, Des?'

'Well, I'll have to buzz round for some more subs,' said Telford. 'Stick your names down.—Thirty bob, did you say, Des?—Well, Darkie?'

'A quid,' answered D'Arcy, taking up his fountain-pen. 'I haven't pinched any medallions lately.'

'Oh, shut up!' Desmond snapped, for he had ceased to joke about the theft now.

But, nevertheless, that subscription list as it went round increased the gossip. And Allerick evidently began to see the trend of the horrible talk. He grew more rough and ungracious than ever, never explained himself, and was avoided by most people except O'Shane. It was only because O'Shane, quick enough to take offence on occasion, simply wouldn't notice Allerick's rudeness, that the captain of Wright's had any chum left. Hare, though much too gentlemanly to join in the talk against Allerick, and still maintaining that he never 'judged anyone,' preferred people who were polite, and after testing Allerick's temper once or twice, withdrew, half-smiling in his own peculiar fashion.

'The point is,' said the Tiger to Desmond, on the Friday morning, 'that no one will call a general prefects' meeting.'

'A what?' asked Desmond, looking up at Telford from the deep grass where he had lazily stretched himself to gaze at the cloudless sky.

'A general prefects' meeting,' answered Telford steadily. 'There is such a thing, you know.'

'Jove! So there is,' Desmond cried, hauling himself into a sitting position. 'Do you know, Tiger, I'd pretty well forgotten that fact.'

'To tell the truth, I had myself,' replied the Tiger, laughing. 'One gets so used to scrappy House meetings, and Wright's and School, or Leigh's and School. It just shows how the business has been soaked into us, so to speak. But I dragged out an old copy of the "Prefects' Rules" to blow the fire up with, and number eight hit me in the eye: "The captain of any House is privileged to call a meeting of the captains and prefects of the other Houses, provided the School-captain is able to be present."'

Desmond's eyes glowed. 'I say, Tiger, you've got more brains than all of us put together. Why, man, that's just what's wanted.'

'Perhaps,' said Telford; 'but don't you think a meeting of that kind might be a bit risky?'

'Risky? How d'you mean?'

'Well, just think. There hasn't been such a thing for ages—Leigh's and Wright's discussing matters. Don't you think the prefects'll be referees before the meeting's over?'

'Let 'em!' Desmond cried. 'I'm going to call a meeting straight off. It's time there was an end to all this scrappy messing.' He suddenly noticed D'Arcy crossing the field, clipping the heads of dandelions off with his tennis racquet. 'Here, Darkie!'

''Lo, Des! Haven't seen you since last night. How are things? Don't you think they might cut the sides of the field as well as the middle? But I suppose the sale of the balls lost in the jungle helps to keep up the School funds?—Hullo, Tiger! Washed your neck lately? I dare say——'

'Do dry up a sec, Darkie, and lend me your fountain-pen,' Desmond interrupted.

'With pleasure,' D'Arcy answered, handing him a fat fountain-pen, carved rather blatantly with the name 'D. Lestrange.' 'I say, Tiger, did you see that glorious bat in the hall?'

'Yes, rather; an absolute ripper.—Did you, Des?'

'Don't interrupt me,' growled Desmond, biting the end of the pen and surveying his hieroglyphic-like writing rather dubiously.

'Of course, you know who it was sent to, don't you, Tiger?' asked D'Arcy.

'No; I didn't care to look for the address.'

'Well, it was Rix's.'

'Eh, what?' Desmond looked up. 'What's that about Rix?'

'He's been buying a dream of a bat, that's all,' D'Arcy answered. 'Worth about five quid.'

'How do I care how much it was worth?' snapped Desmond. ''Pon my word, I don't know why you fellows don't keep a book and put Allerick's expenses down as they come. There's his jam, and his socks and ties. It'd be easier to add up.'

'We don't believe any of the yarns about Allerick, you know jolly well,' answered the

Tiger. 'But I do wish, for his own sake, Allerick'd say where his sudden wealth came from.'

'His Auntie Mabel's dead, of course,' Desmond said.

'His what? Didn't know he had an Auntie Mabel.'

'He hasn't, for all I know,' grinned Desmond. 'Pull me up, Darkie! I say, will this do: "A general meeting of prefects is to be held in the School House common-room at seven-thirty this evening, Friday. S. Loring will preside.—Signed, N. Desmond"?'

'Sounds all right, Des,' answered Darkie; 'but will Loring agree?'

'See Rule number eight,' smiled Desmond. 'He can't very well refuse if he's free. And if he can't come this evening, I'll jolly well call another on Monday. Come on, I'll go to Loring now.'

'Get your racquet and have a set with me now, Tiger,' commanded Darkie. 'We've got nearly half an hour before third lesson.'

'Righto,' agreed the Tiger. 'I think Loring's sitting on the form outside the baths, Des.'

'Is he? Thanks. Cheerio. I'll come round to you afterwards.' He made his way across the field to the big white glass-roofed building.

Sure enough, Loring was sitting there alone, a book on his knee. But he was not reading, nor was he watching the keen practice of the Second Eleven. He was thinking deeply and frowning. Loring was a very clever chap, and his cleverness cut him off from his fellows to a great extent. Moreover, where Classics were concerned he was a genius—and a genius should never be made School-captain. He liked to be the centre of the School, but he liked better to be in a quiet corner with a book. Now his responsibility as School-captain had taken hold of him, and prevented him from reading, and he greeted the captain of Leigh's with an air of relief. 'Why, Desmond, you're just the chap I wanted to see. I was going to look for you. I—as a matter of fact, it's about something I can't very well discuss with anyone less than a captain— and . . .'

Desmond sat down, and Loring noticed the paper in his hand. 'Is your business important?' he asked. 'What is it?'

'Oh, only this,' answered Desmond, handing him the paper. Loring deciphered the notice, and seemed a little astonished.

'Rule number eight, you know,' explained Desmond. 'Are you free this evening, Loring?'

'Well, I am, but . . . Look here, it's this way. The Head's just told me something about that medallion, and he told me to tell you, and also Allerick. I'll tell you now; but you'll see when I've told you, how jolly difficult it is to tell Rix. I don't know whether the Head jumped to it, or even whether he knows what's going on in Wright's. . . . You get me, don't you?'

'I do!' replied Desmond grimly.

'Well, it's this way—come round the corner, I don't want anyone to hear—the Head started looking for the medallion with the thought of what the thief would do with it, see? And he guessed that a public school-boy would try to sell it, and couldn't sell it in London, so would look for somewhere round here. And that led him to that queer little jeweller's in Trelthorpe Lane—you know, Dowling's?'

'Rather,' answered Desmond, and catching the School-captain's eye, he knew that he too had heard Horton's tale.

'Well, old Dowling, on hearing a description of the thing, said he'd had it offered to him three days ago. He hadn't taken it, and he wouldn't give any reason for his refusal to buy it. Probably he thought it was a bit fishy. The Head asked who had taken it there. Old Dowling started to mumble something about being short-sighted, which, by the way, I doubt. But in the end he let out one or two facts about the chap.'

'Well?' Desmond's eyes were dark with excitement, he twisted the notice about in his big hands. Loring spoke even lower, and there was a kind of hoarseness in his voice.

'One, that he was on the short side; two, that he had dark hair; three, that he had a brown trilby hat, pulled down over his eyes; four, that he had either a black or a dark navy mac; and five, he—he —er—er— horn-rimmed spectacles.'

'Specs? I say . . .' Desmond sprang from the seat and stood facing Loring. 'Do you think . . . There's no use beating about the bush, is there?' he whispered. 'Do you think it'll be news to Rix? I mean—I mean, do you believe what chaps are saying about Rix?'

'No,' answered Loring without hesitation. 'I'd trust Rix with my last shilling. But there's no one else in the School as dark as he is, and he's the only chap who wears

"Harold Lloyds." I wish to goodness old Dowling could remember the exact date the chap went to the shop, but the old scarecrow can't—or won't. It's jolly rotten for Allerick, and I'm hanged if I know how I'm going to tell him. But the Head said, "Tell Desmond and Allerick, but please don't let it get over the School, as yet. The prefects may know, if you think it won't go any further." Well, why didn't the Newt want it to become common property? If you ask me, he's seen what we see——'

'A picture of Rix crawling about in a turned-down trilby and a black mac, do you mean?' broke in Desmond. 'No, thank you; it doesn't seem to fit in with things, thank you.'

'Can you tell Rix?'

'I can't. He won't let me near him. There was—a—a—misunderstanding about a fortnight ago, at the time when their museum was messed up——'

'I see——' Loring smiled wearily.

'You think you do,' Desmond replied. 'But, anyway, my face seems to annoy Rix.'

'That's the worst of it—most things seem to annoy him nowadays. If only he would keep his temper—but then, would we under the circumstances? I'm not so sure. Which

would be best, Desmond; just to tell him as
it were a message from the Head, or to
admit what had jumped into your head at
the description?'

'Oh, don't try to bluff,' Desmond advised.
'Rix is much too sharp. No; I'd tell him,
and let him face it how he likes. But I
won't be a witness of the scene.'

'Do you funk it?' Loring asked.

'No,' replied Desmond steadily; 'but I'm
not going to try Rix's sweet regard for me
for the third time. And as for this—well . . .'
He tore the notice into fragments, which the
wind scattered like small butterflies among
the long grass.

CHAPTER VII.

THE MEDALLION IS FOUND.

So there was no general prefects' meeting. But at Wright's there was a meeting which had very startling results. It took the strange form of a prefects' meeting without the captain. Nobody knew exactly who called it, but the prefects of Wright's found themselves in the common-room on Thursday evening, discussing Allerick with great heat. O'Shane was not there, of course—it would not be safe to have him, and Hare was such a queer chap, one felt sure he wouldn't discuss anyone behind his back, even though it were for the good of the School. The leader of the conversation appeared to be Robson. The rich boy sat on the table, cool and dignified, and King, Spencer, Gregory, Cairns, and Collins lolled in various positions on chairs around him.

'The matter has gone so far now,' Robson was saying, 'that it must be cleared up one way or the other.'

'Yes, but how to do it?' inquired Spencer, a hatchet-faced fellow, with pale yellow hair, the coarse texture of which caused him to be known as 'Straw.' 'There don't seem to be many helpful suggestions flying round.'

'Well, this is how it is,' Robson went on, his grey eyes very serious: 'most of us suspect Allerick of having pinched the medallion . . .' There was a rather uneasy stir among the others. The door was slightly open, Collins rose and closed it firmly. Robson passed a well-manicured hand over his shining fair hair and smiled almost apologetically. 'It's a rotten thing to admit that the captain of a fine House like Wright's is a common thief, but there it is. We don't know everything, it's the motive that counts—the need. We know poor old Allerick is—er—*was* jolly hard up, and——'

'Is there any need for the sermon, Robbie?' cut in Cairns in his direct way. 'I don't remember Allerick having a starving wife and twelve ragged children. Stealing's stealing, whether a chap's on the rocks or rolling. No need to preach.'

For a moment Robson looked very angry at the interruption, then his flashing smile broke out again. 'Oh well, perhaps not,' he answered quietly. 'I don't want to waste time any more than you chaps do, but as I said, this thing must be cleared up one way or the other. We can't have such a—a—cloud hanging over us. It gives fellows a chance to call us . . . It gives a handle to Leigh's——'

'Well, what can we *do*?' It was King who interrupted this time. 'We can't very well demand a thorough search of all his possessions.'

'No — that's true,' said Robson, very slowly; 'but we could . . .' He hesitated and frowned. 'No—perhaps it wouldn't do,' he added.

'What wouldn't do?' queried King impatiently.

Robson didn't answer, and Cairns, who had guessed his thoughts, went on. 'There's such a thing as an unauthorised search.'

'A what?' asked Spencer. 'Do you mean, we could search without Allerick knowing?'

'Allerick would have to know,' Robson said. 'Unless . . . Do you think, supposing Allerick *had* the medallion, he'd keep it in his study?'

'No,' answered Spencer.

'Hasn't he sold the thing, of course?

broke in Cairns. 'That's why he's rolling all of a sudden.'

'But there's probably in his study some proof of the theft,' Robson continued.

'Oh, I'm sick of this, you fellows!' Cairns said. 'Why doesn't somebody ask Allerick to his face if he's stolen it?'

'You do it,' suggested Robson, with a malicious little smile.

'Well, if everyone's afraid of his anger, they can't really be certain he stole the medallion,' Cairns asserted. 'I have my doubts.'

'Then you shouldn't be here,' Robson said. 'This is a meeting of chaps who believe Allerick to be guilty. No, it's no use talking of confronting Allerick. We must act before he suspects our movements, that's all.'

'Then why *not* search his study?' asked Spencer.

'It'd be better than jawing for hours together,' added Cairns.

'But what price old Pat O'Shane?' asked King thoughtfully. 'We've got to reckon with him.'

'We'll have to get him out of the way,' said Gregory. 'He's dead nuts on Allerick, and wouldn't stand for any searching, you bet.'

'O'Shane is foolish,' Robson answered.

'He must see how suspicious Allerick's behaviour is. And Allerick isn't pleasant with him, anyway. I 've heard him say some rotten things to O'Shane. I wouldn't stand for it, but O'Shane 's queer. These Irish, you know, you never get them.'

'Thanks, Robbie,' put in Collins.

'Oh, present company excepted, of course,' Robson said. 'Anyway, you aren't blind, Collins; which O'Shane appears to be. Well, then, we 've decided to search, have we? Hands up for those in favour.'

After some hesitation all hands went up. Robson slipped from the table and stood stiffly before them. In the fading sunlight his hair shone like polished metal, his profile's shadow on the yellow-painted wall almost showed the supercilious curl of his lip, his up-tilted chin. Amongst this small company of schoolboys he was the only one who stood out as striking. It was not only his wealth nor his handsome appearance which made him their leader, but a strength of personality which discounted his contemptuous air and arrogant carriage. 'That 's unanimous,' he said. 'There 's nothing else to consider, except Hare.'

'On Saturday,' Gregory said, 'Hare is going across to Calleridge for the day. If

Allerick and O'Shane go off anywhere on Saturday evening, then's our chance.'

'So it is,' Robson answered. 'We can't do anything till then, anyway—it's out of the question. So be ready on Saturday evening if called upon, you chaps.'

'It doesn't take six people to search one small study,' said Cairns, who seemed less pleased than the others with the arrangement.

'That's true, I know,' Robson answered, taking the lead again as a matter of course. 'But suppose we get called over the coals over it, which is quite likely, then it'll look better if there was a regular body. And you can't get away from the fact that we're all the Sixth, except O'Shane, Hare, and Allerick.'

'Which is two-thirds, to be precise,' Cairns replied. 'Well, why be called over the coals? If we get evidence of Allerick's guilt we're justified; if not, say no more about it.'

'That certainly seems sensible,' Robson murmured. 'Well, that's clear enough, anyway. Keep on the lookout for a clue to Allerick's arrangements for Saturday.'

'Righto!' was the answer, and the meeting broke up. Next day, Spencer was in the gym at the same time as Allerick and O'Shane, and

heard Allerick ungraciously accept the Irishman's invitation to go for a long cycle-ride to
Netherlowe Woods on the Saturday afternoon.

'I'll mug you tea at that little shack in
the copse,' promised O'Shane. 'And it'll
blow the cobwebs off you a bit, old bean.'

Spencer hurried hot-foot to tell Robson,
who smiled, and sent the message round to
the other four. Thus it was on Saturday
afternoon they did not leave the School
grounds, but stayed practising at the nets
until four-thirty; then Robson started to stroll
into Wright's House, and one by one the
others followed him, carefully, for fear any of
the Staff noticed, and a few minutes later they
were all inside Study 3, with the door locked.

The room which Allerick shared with
O'Shane was bigger than the others belonging to Wright's, and was reserved always
for the captain and whichever of his chums
he delighted to honour. It was bright and
well-furnished, with three oak chairs, a roll-
top desk, and two cupboards, while cases
and boxes of various kinds were arranged
carelessly around the walls.

'Do a cupboard, Greg,' ordered Robson;
'and Spencer and I'll look through this
desk.'

Cairns did not help with the search, but

stood in the centre of the room, watching. He saw Spencer open one of the drawers at the side of the desk, and turn over the papers in it. Then he picked something up, and continued to stare at it.

'What's that, Straw?' Cairns asked. 'We're looking for the medallion, you know.' He thought it was enough to overhaul Allerick's possessions like that without taking a sneaking interest in them.

'It'll be something of Pat O'Shane's, this. It can't belong to Allerick.'

'What is it?' asked Robson, looking up from the writing-case in which he was burrowing. Spencer passed it to him. It was a photograph of a pretty girl, with curling dark hair and a roguish smile. She was clad in a gym-tunic, and carried a hockey-stick. It was inscribed 'Eileen to Bruce.'

'As I happen to know O'Shane's name is Pat,' Robson remarked, 'that belongs to Allerick. Put it back, Straw; we're not here to spy on Allerick's love affairs. She's got rotten taste, that's all.'

Spencer put the photograph back reluctantly, and was about to open another drawer when Robson gave an exclamation.

'What's up?' asked Cairns, striding forward, and the others looked round. Robson merely

moved aside, and they saw what had caused
his cry. He had opened a small tin, inscribed
' 40 nibs,' in the writing-case, and there, just
placed carelessly within, was the Necra medallion. Without its plush case it looked even
more wonderful than before. Its sixty tiny
rubies sparkled and glowed as if it delighted
in the mischief it had caused. The six boys
gazed at it in silence, then Cairns said slowly,
' I   say—poor   old   Allerick !   So   it   was
him !'

' There 's no need to be sorry for him,'
Collins snapped. ' Think of the School, man,
think of the School.'

' St Martin's reputation is saved, anyway,'
Robson said ; ' the police hadn't to be called
in.   Straighten the place up, and then we 'll
take this mischievous bit of jewellery to Dr
Newton.'   He was very calm and controlled,
but then Robson always was.   The other
five were flushed or trembling with excitement, he alone picked up the medallion as
though it were merely an india-rubber, or
something else commonplace and usual, and
closed up the writing-case.   Come along,' he
said, and led the way out of the study.

' I wonder what the Newt 'll say ?' Cairns
murmured, as they went along the passage
to the Head's room.

'You'll soon know,' Collins answered without enthusiasm.

The Head seemed surprised to see them all troop in when he called 'Come in.' 'What's this?' he inquired, smiling. 'A deputation?'

Robson showed at that moment his love of staginess. He walked impressively up to the desk and, without a word of introduction, placed the Necra medallion on the centre of the white blotter before the Head-master.

Dr Newton sprang to his feet as though he had been stung. He gazed at the medallion as though he could scarcely believe his eyes. 'The Necra medallion! I—boys . . . Where did you find this, Robson?'

Robson paused, then he spoke in a low voice, as if he had some difficulty in getting out the words. 'In Allerick's writing-case, sir,' he answered at last.

'In—Allerick's—writing—case?' The Head repeated the words as though he scarcely grasped them. His face became set and hard. 'I had hoped that there was some other explanation than theft, after all,' he said slowly. 'But it appears that one of the most trusted members of St Martin's is the culprit.'

Then another thought crossed his mind. He looked directly at Robson, his eyes cold.

' How came you to be searching in Allerick's writing-case ? ' asked he.

' We had decided, sir,' Robson answered, 'that the evidence against Allerick was overwhelming, and thought we were justified in making certain. We acted for the sake of our House, sir.'

' And why, may I ask,' pursued the Head, ' did you not place the matter before me ? '

' We did not consider it necessary, sir,' Robson answered quietly, but with supreme self-confidence. ' We are all prefects.'

' You were a little presumptuous, I think, boys,' the Head-master replied. ' But, anyway, the medallion is found, and the School's honour is saved. You may go. Thank you.'

They went, not feeling very pleased with themselves.

' He didn't seem very grateful, I noticed,' Cairns commented.

' He 's jolly well relieved to see that medallion again, all the same,' Robson said. ' I don't regret for a moment my share in the matter. Who knows, Allerick may have got rid of the thing next week, sold it or something, and then it 'd have been too late.'

' Poor old Allerick,' Cairns said again. ' I wonder what he 'll do now ? '

'You're wasting a lot of sympathy on the fellow,' Collins said. 'Why, he's pretty hard-faced. Fancy anyone stampeding round as he has the last few days, and all the time having the medallion in his desk.'

'I can't understand it,' Cairns said. 'Even now I . . .' He did not finish his sentence, but started whistling half-heartedly.

'You ought to be glad the thing's turned up,' Collins said. 'Allerick won't be any loss to the School. He's swimming-captain, of course; but plenty of chaps will make as good a captain of swimming. And we'll get somebody better for the First Eleven.'

'The Newt didn't say he'd expel him.'

'He didn't say anything about what he was going to do to the thief at all,' Robson put in. 'But, of course, he'll be expelled.'

'What a blot on Wright's!' Gregory exclaimed. 'Leigh's have got the pull over us in this, anyway.'

'I believe Desmond tried to chum up with Allerick, anyway,' Spencer said; 'but Allerick snubbed him pretty awfully.'

'No credit to Desmond,' King answered. 'Just shows his rotten taste.'

Cairns ceased his dismal rendering of the 'Londonderry Air,' and turned on the others almost fiercely. 'Perhaps my memory may be going wunky,' he snapped, 'but I seem to remember you were all jolly chummy with Allerick at one time—and not so long ago either.'

'We all make mistakes,' Robson replied sententiously. 'We're as surprised as you that Allerick's turned out such a rotter, but there's no need for you to get so heated about things. Anybody'd think you were defending the fellow.'

'And perhaps I am,' retorted Cairns. 'I'll say this. It'd have to be a pretty good reason that'd make a chap like him steal.'

Robson stared at him for a moment, then he shrugged his broad shoulders and laughed lightly. 'Oh well, Cairns,' he answered, 'if this has hit you, think of O'Shane and Hare, who trusted Allerick all through; they'll get a shock. We'll have to be more careful in our choice of captain, that's all.'

'Yes; I wonder who it will be?' King went on.

'There's no need to discuss that until Allerick's finally gone, is there?' Robson asked, with a slight frown. 'Better wait till Allerick's gone, eh?' But there was a glint in his grey eyes, which Cairns noticed.

'Robbie thinks he's going to be captain in Allerick's place,' Cairns whispered to

Gregory, as they dropped behind the others in the quadrangle.

'Well, why not?' asked Gregory. 'He's the best chap we've got, and he'll know how to stand up to Leigh's.'

'Oh, Leigh's! Leigh's! Leigh's!' groaned Cairns; 'I'm sick of the sound of the word.'

'We all are,' Gregory retorted; 'but we can't let them walk over us.'

'Why not?'

'Go and run the tap over your head!' Gregory advised rudely. 'You're wandering!'

CHAPTER VIII.

THE HEAD'S DECISION.

'TIME to go back, Pat,' Allerick said lazily.

'Och, that's so,' O'Shane murmured, raising himself on his elbow and glancing at his watch. 'Four-thirty.'

'And I'm jolly hungry,' announced Allerick, as he rose and brushed bits of gorse and grass from his coat. 'It's rotten of that beastly tea-shop to be closed.'

'It is, sure, Rix,' O'Shane agreed. 'I'd not have brought you here if I'd thought we'd have to go back for tea. It's not worth while.'

'Well, I'm not sorry we came, Pat,' Allerick said. 'It's jolly nice and quiet here, and you know when to jaw and when to shut up. I hate chaps who drivel on all the bally day.'

'You're not a talkative bird, certainly, Rix, and you've a beastly temper. Sometimes I wonder why I put up with you.' O'Shane laughed, and dragged his bicycle up.

Allerick stooped down to fasten his shoe,

and therefore his voice was rather muffled as he answered unexpectedly, 'You can't wonder more than I do, Pat.'

O'Shane was slightly alarmed, this was such a lot for Allerick to admit. 'Rot!' he laughed; 'there are worse fellows than you, B. D. Allerick.'

'I dare say,' Allerick retorted; 'but they don't get anyone to stick to them like you stick to me.'

'Oh, dry up!' O'Shane murmured. 'I wouldn't do it if it didn't suit me. You overestimate my loyalty.'

'You're not deaf, Pat.'

'What d'you mean?'

'You've heard what the chaps are saying.'

'For Mike's sake, Rix, don't start on that again. I wish the filthy medallion were at the bottom of the sea!'

'Much good that'd do. Well, I'll let the matter drop. Hold this while I tie the camera on. What are you grinning at?'

'Nothing, I mean——'

''Pon my word, I can't understand you— oh, dash it——'

'Here, I'll do it,' O'Shane said, for Allerick's hands were trembling with impatience. 'You should keep your hair on, Rix.'

They mounted the bicycles and set off again down the long, dusty road. Neither of them spoke for a long while, then Allerick said, 'I say, Pat!'

'Yes?' O'Shane drew up to Allerick. 'What is it?'

'What do you think would happen if I resigned the captaincy?'

'Resign the captaincy? What on earth for?'

'I wish you'd answer a question when you're asked one!' Allerick snapped irritably. 'I didn't say I was going to resign. I asked you what you thought would happen if I *did* resign.'

'You shouldn't spring these things on a chap suddenly. Anyway, I dare say the new captain'd be a surprise-packet, like Desmond was.'

'Weren't you expecting Desmond to be captain of Leigh's?'

'No; I put my shilling on Lestrange. Decent chap, Lestrange; but Desmond is the best of the bunch.'

'Everyone to their own opinion,' Allerick growled.

'Rot,' laughed O'Shane. 'You know you're as cracked on Desmond as I am.'

For a moment Allerick looked quite

murderous. 'Me? Why, I hate the fellow!' he asserted.

'Rot!' repeated O'Shane, unperturbed. 'Silly rot!'

'What did Desmond want with you that morning when you called on him?'

'Don't be so beastly inquisitive,' O'Shane answered, but he coloured a little. 'You wouldn't tell me what he wanted the night before.'

'Same thing, I suppose,' Allerick growled. 'He's a hypocrite.'

'You know he's not,' O'Shane answered quietly. 'Don't be an ass, Rix. And don't talk about resigning the captaincy. You're the best man in Wright's for the job; and we don't want anyone, like Gregory, who'll think of nothing but rotting Leigh's. Not that Gregory's not a jolly decent chap, of course, but he's better as a prefect.'

They drew near to the School gates, and outside there were a crowd of fellows talking. As the two jumped from their bicycles and started to wheel them to the shed, a dead silence fell over the group. O'Shane noticed it, and turned to Allerick. Allerick's face was set and expressionless. So it had come to this!

As they entered the shed Hare drew up

to them. 'Hullo!' said he. 'Had a decent time?'

'We have—yes,' Allerick answered in a tone more cordial than Hare had heard him use for a week. 'It was topping in the copse.'

'Only we couldn't get any grub, so we're absolutely famished.—Stick your bike here, Rix, there's room,' O'Shane added. Then as he went out he turned to Hare and said, 'What are those fellows at the gate staring at, Whiskers? Do we *look* extra queer?'

'I don't know,' said Hare, without meaning any insult. He looked worried. He had not heard the startling news, of course, being away all day, but he had heard somebody say: 'Well it's good-bye to Allerick, anyway,' as he passed that group, and it wasn't a pleasant thing to hear. 'It'll be some new queer yarn they've got hold of,' he added, looking quickly at Allerick. 'Some chaps'd believe anything.'

Together they walked into the building, and hardly had they set foot inside the passage than Seddon approached them, serious and important. 'Mr Allerick,' he said, 'Dr Newton wishes to see you at once.'

Allerick paled slightly, not because it was strange for the Head to send for him, but because he knew instinctively that there was something wrong. He shrank inwardly, but his expression did not change. 'Right, Seddon,' he replied.—'I'll see you in a few minutes, Pat. For mercy's sake, get a good spread-out, or I'll be eating the Head.'

O'Shane laughed, but he gave Allerick's arm a quick little squeeze before he went, for he too had a premonition of evil.

When Allerick reached the Head's study he stood outside for a moment and half-closed his eyes. If he was praying, his prayer was: 'Oh, let me keep my temper; don't let me lose my temper.' He knew as sure as that he stood there that something had happened, and he remembered the scene in the hall after the theft of the medallion. He must be calm; he must be calm. He knocked at the beautiful carved door.

'Come in!' called the Head, and Allerick entered. Then it was easy to be calm. The soft evening sunshine fell across the grey carpet and the polished desk, lit up the inscrutable marble face of Dante and the black wave of the Head-master's head as he bent over the desk. Allerick stood there, waiting, looking down at the raven hair, and gaining a strange courage from it. There was not a grey thread in it, and it meant that the Head was young. Why did he feel so glad that the Head was young? But Allerick was afraid, and when the Head raised his eyes he knew that his fear was justified.

'Allerick,' commenced Dr Newton, and stopped.

'Yes, sir,' answered the captain of Wright's, and then again there was silence. The Head-master took a key from his pocket and opened the drawer in the desk, taking out a small leather case. He snapped open the case, and the Necra medallion flashed upon Allerick with all its sixty red eyes. Allerick opened his mouth to speak, then closed it again. Relief welled up in his heart, and sank again at the Head's next words.

'This was found in your writing-case, Allerick. Have you anything to say?'

Was Allerick a supreme actor, wondered the Head, that the surprise in his ugly face appeared so genuine? But it was succeeded by the wild glare of rage so frequently seen in Allerick's eyes. The boy felt his control going, and made a sudden successful effort to be calm. 'I—didn't put it there,' he answered at last.

'Then who did? Who shares your study? O'Shane?'

'O'Shane hasn't anything to do with it, sir,' Allerick answered swiftly. 'He was talking to Lord Inverslowe when the medallion was stolen. I don't know how it came in my writing-case.'

The Head rose. He came and confronted Allerick, and placed his hands on the boy's shoulders. 'Allerick,' he asked, 'did you steal the Necra medallion?'

Allerick felt weary and persecuted. He was sick of the Necra medallion. He could not defend himself. He looked up into the Head's searching blue eyes and answered, 'No, sir.'

'Do you *know* who stole it?'

'No, sir.' He dropped his head on to his chest, his shoulders hunched.

The Head smiled. 'I *am* glad, Allerick. I think I'd rather *anyone* a thief than you.'

Allerick looked up, and could hardly believe the smile. 'Do you mean . . . are you . . . Oh, sir, are you going to take my word for it?'

'Of course, Allerick. Isn't your word good? I've always found it so. Sit down, my boy, and let's try to fathom a little of this mystery.'

Allerick dropped almost weakly into the nearest chair. It was as though a great cloud had been lifted from over him. 'I never thought . . . It *does* look as though I'd stolen it. I don't know anything about it, sir.'

'Allerick, you're getting a better man,' the Head smiled. 'Do you know, you'd have been too proud to deny anything a little while ago? But you've had a rough time, and also I'm afraid you're in for one, my boy. Now, will you answer a few questions for me?'

'Yes, sir.'

'What did you purchase or sell at Dowling's last week?'

The colour rushed into Allerick's sallow face. 'A—a—collarette, sir; a lace collar.'

'Oh?' The Head-master cleverly dissembled his surprise. 'For your mother, no doubt?'

'No, sir.' Allerick's eyes were studying the thick carpet. 'For Eileen O'Shane.'

'O'Shane's sister?'

'Yes, sir.'

'Well, that's very jolly,' the Head-master went on, with a whimsical half-smile, 'to write to your friend's sister. Is she at school too?'

'Yes, sir; Venderlea. She's hockey-captain.'

If anyone had told Allerick that he could have sat calmly talking of Eileen O'Shane to Dr Newton he would have hurled ridicule at him. Yet here he was, in the light of those clear blue eyes, feeling calmer and happier than he had been for many days.

'That's explained, then,' the Head said. 'I see why you didn't want Sikes to over-hear your deal. I sha'n't tell anyone, Allerick.'

'Thank you, sir.' For the first time during the interview Allerick smiled, and it was quite wonderful how much more like-able his smile made him.

'And do you mind telling me, Allerick, how it is you are—er—in funds just at present?'

Allerick hesitated for a moment, then he said, 'My uncle has decided to pay my fees to Oxford, sir, if I will go out to Egypt with him when I am twenty-two. I wanted to go to Cambridge, you know, but I accepted his offer when I failed in the scholarship examination. He was very pleased, and gave me a cheque for ten pounds. He's very wealthy. My *funds* are spent now. It was only the new bat and the five-pound sub for the hospital which gave rise to the rumour that I was suddenly well-off.'

'You were very generous to give half your tip in subscription, Allerick.'

'Oh no, sir,' replied Allerick almost curtly; 'I didn't want anything except the bat, sir. I don't believe in money, sir.'

The Head smiled and shook his head. 'I can't help being amused at a Communist who studies violently for a State scholarship, and goes to Oxford at a rich uncle's expense.'

Allerick flushed. He was quite serious over his Communism. 'I want to learn, so that I'll be better equipped to help the cause, sir.'

'Well, it's good to have ideals, mistaken or no. And perhaps you're not mistaken, Allerick. Carry on, my boy. But about this medallion. You must have an enemy. O'Shane is out of the question, you say—so . . . I wonder, could one of the Sixth-form boys have put the medallion where it was found? Spencer—Gregory—Cairns—King—Collins—Robson? No. We can only return the treasure to its owner, and wait for a solution of the mystery. Well, go now, Allerick; you look tired and hungry. When did you have tea?'

'I haven't had it yet, sir.'

'You foolish boy! Why didn't you let me know?'

'It's all right, sir. O'Shane'll have it ready for me.'

'Will he? That's good. Hurry off, then. Good-night, Allerick.' He held out his hand.

'Good-night, sir,' Allerick said, grasping it.

'Come to me if things get difficult, you know. Good-night.'

Allerick strode along the passage with erect head and glowing eyes. He was even glad he had been accused of stealing the medallion, because it had been the means of his discovery of this wonderful Dr Newton. What did he care for the School? His word was good enough for the best Head-master in the world. He kicked open the door of the study.

O'Shane was just pouring the boiling water into the tea-pot. He looked round, and his thin smiling face was hot and damp from bending over the fire. 'Whew! What an age you've been, Rix!'

'You needn't have waited. Oh, I say, muffins!'

'I popped over to the tuck-hole for them.'

'You old sport! Jove! I've got an appetite.'

'You look awfully bucked. What did the Newt want?'

'A committee of interfering asses took it upon themselves to search this study.'

'What?' O'Shane's eyes became wide. 'The cheeky blighters! What did they expect to find?'

'The medallion, of course.'

'Of all the——' O'Shane nearly upset his tea in his indignation. 'My giddy aunt!'

'The funny part about it is,' Allerick went on, speaking with his mouth full of muffin, and, to his astonishment, quite enjoying the changing expressions on the Irishman's face, 'they did find it.'

O'Shane laughed derisively. 'I *thought* you were rotting,' he grunted comfortably. 'You old owl!'

'I was never more serious in my life,' Allerick answered. 'How they did it, I don't know; but they found the beastly thing reposing quietly in the old leather writing-case I pinched from old Maycott last term.'

'But who put it there?' O'Shane stammered. 'I don't get you. Who'd had the writing-case?'

'No one; it was in the desk.'

'But *you* didn't put the thing in it, Rix.'

'No, old bean.'

'Well, what's the Newt going to do? I—how . . . Goodness, Rix, surely he can't——'

'He asked me if I pinched the medallion, and just simply believed me when I said I didn't, that's all.'

'But who could . . . I say, Rix, this is all beyond me. All the Sixth except Hare searched here?'

'Yes.'

'The rotters! Upon my word, you never

know people until something like this happens.
They don't believe in you, then?'

'No. I don't care.'

'It'll be a blow for them to find the
Head's a chap who'll take one's word. The
prying asses! Well, I'm glad the rotten
medallion's found. I was thinking seriously
of having a fake one done to turn up in its
place. I wouldn't be too pleased, Rix. Even
now, things are going to be rough if these
chaps aren't going to admit their mistake.'

'Perhaps one can't blame them,' Allerick
murmured—for the muffins and marmalade
had put him in a good humour with all the
world. 'The evidence is alarmingly overwhelming.'

'But there's you,' O'Shane answered vaguely.
'You're the best evidence. They know you.'
He lapsed into thoughtful silence, and studied
Allerick's thin figure from head to toe.

Allerick was leaning against the mantel-
piece, drumming idly on it with his fingers.
'What are you staring at, you great goof?'
he asked.

'I was thinking,' O'Shane murmured, 'that
perhaps, after all, they don't.'

'I don't know what on earth you're drivel-
ling about,' Allerick grunted. 'What about
doing a bit of work?'

'I can't bear the thought of it. Anyway, there's not much time. Come for a stroll round.'

They went, and met Hare immediately outside. He was worried and annoyed. 'I say, Rix, isn't this awful? What are you going to do?' he asked.

Allerick told him about the Head's decision.

The cloud of anxiety cleared from Hare's face. 'That's jolly decent,' he said. 'But it's rotten for you, Rix. Somebody's framed this up against you. Do you know of anyone who dislikes you?'

'No,' answered Allerick; 'at least, not enough for that.'

They turned the corner of the building, arm-in-arm, and bumped heavily into someone.

'Sorry!' a gruff voice put in. It was Desmond. O'Shane smiled broadly, and Hare followed suit, with a 'Good-night, Desmond!' Desmond smiled back, but his smile was directed towards Allerick. Allerick felt he could like even the hateful, handsome captain of Leigh's this evening. He smiled back.

'Had a decent day?' asked Desmond.

'Ripping, thanks,' answered O'Shane. 'Have you?'

'Rather! I—oh, never mind!' Desmond

said, as he gave Allerick a final look and turned away.

'By the way,' Hare said, 'I heard some-one telling Desmond about this business, Rix.'

'Oh?' Allerick tried not to look interested, but he could not deny to himself that he was.

'And Desmond said the Newt knew a straight chap when he saw one, and they'd be sold if they expected you to be packing. He seemed so jolly confident about it. Not that he shouldn't have been—but—Leigh's—you know . . .' His sentence drifted away.

Allerick did not answer. He wanted to forget about Desmond, and he found it the most difficult task in the world.

CHAPTER IX.

THE SCHOOL'S DECISION.

TO say that the School was surprised when the Head-master trusted Allerick would but be a mild way of describing its feelings. Everyone, except those who had known and liked Allerick for years, considered him as guilty as if he had been caught with the medallion in his hands. And they spared no pains to let him know this. When Allerick went into the Sixth-form pew on the Sunday morning he had empty spaces on each side of him, until Hare and O'Shane quietly walked across to fill them up. Robson looked round with an expression of the deepest disgust, but Allerick took no notice. In any case, he had no use for a chap who would lead an underhand search-party.

In the sermon, which was on 'Brotherhood,' the chaplain dealt with tolerance and with generosity towards the faults of others. He said people were often too swift to judge, too logical, and too apt to stick to

their opinions ruthlessly. The sermon might
have been made specially for the occasion,
but it had no affect on Allerick's erstwhile
friends. When he spoke to them they were
deaf, having evidently decided to send him
to Coventry.

O'Shane was amused. Coventry, shared
by Hare and himself, with occasional visits
from Desmond, and the Head-master in
the background, appeared a not undesirable
residence. 'You said you hated chaps to
be always jawing at you, Rix,' said he.
'Here's where you're going to have the
time of your life.'

Allerick laughed dryly. 'Those five without Robson would be sheep without a shep-
herd,' he said. 'Robson's the big noise.'

'Poor old Robbie!' O'Shane said, with
a little chuckle. 'He'd love to be captain
of Wright's. The dear infant was probably
counting on your being chucked out.'

'Has it ever struck you, you long Antrim
worm,' Allerick put in, 'that they can force
me to resign the captaincy?'

'How can they? They can make it awkward, of course; but you'll stick it out,
won't you, Rix? They'll see their mistake
sooner or later. And surely the medallion
mystery will be cleared up before long.'

'What's the use of a captain who's not obeyed? I can't punish them in a body. They'll render my position useless. Besides, there's the School to think of. There's swimming. We'll lose the swimming race against Leigh's if they won't listen to me. Perhaps it would be better to resign at once.'

'Oh, Rix, you awful ass!'

'But I'm not going to,' finished Allerick 'There's a good strong strain of obstinacy in this child. If I can't make them see reason about the swimming, Leigh's will just have to beat them, that's all. With careful team-work, we could have mopped the floor with Desmond's lot—there's only Lestrange who's a really good swimmer. But if they're going to depend on Robbie to set the pace, and leave me out of the team, it's Wright's that'll be floored. I'm the best swimmer in the School,' Allerick went on, as one stating a well-known fact, 'and they're potty if they reckon without me.'

But that was what the Sixth evidently were doing. When Allerick and his two faithful companions arrived at the baths that afternoon for the final practice before the match, which was to be held next day, they found the other four members of the team, which consisted of Allerick, O'Shane, King, Collins, Robson, and Gregory, swimming up and down furiously.

'You asses, take things quietly,' Allerick called, forgetting all about Coventry in his enthusiasm for swimming. 'Keep your head up, Collins.'

Collins's head went lower if anything. Robson hauled himself out of the water and came to the three. His fair hair hung in dripping curls around his handsome face, and his strong broad shoulders shone like alabaster. 'Get your togs off, Pat,' he said to O'Shane, ignoring Allerick.

'Dear me, how bossy we are this morning,' O'Shane smiled, his blue eyes studying Robson with lazy insolence. 'Do you know, I've a fancy to jump in with my togs *on.*—May I, Rix?'

'Oh, come on,' growled Allerick, marching into the dressing-room. When the door was closed behind them, Robson hailed the other three out of the water. They came, attentive and obedient, as though Robson had the right to command their life and death.

'Look here,' Robson said, 'Allerick's going to be awkward. We're not standing any, are we? Do we want a low-down thief for a swimming-captain?'

'How delicately you word it!' said Cairns, who was watching; but no one took any notice of him.

'Rather not!' Gregory said hotly. 'We can do without him.'

'He's our best swimmer,' Cairns ventured.

'What difference does that make? You're not unsporting enough to want to overlook his character just so's we'll be surer of beating Leigh's, are you?' challenged Robson.

'A rather different definition of "sporting" is needed,' replied Cairns, refusing to argue. 'I can't supply it. But I'm hanged if we'll beat Leigh's without Allerick.'

'We've got to!' Robson asserted. 'Just to show him we don't need chaps like him to pull up our game.' He was so assured, so self-confident, as he stood there, with folded arms and back-flung head, that he seemed to endue the others with some of his spirit. As Allerick, O'Shane, and Hare returned from the dressing-room they lined up almost theatrically beside the rich boy, Hare was still fully dressed; he was not going in, as the baths were wanted clear for the practice, but he was staying to see how the battle went. O'Shane, thinner than ever without his clothes, swung his long arms about, and jumped up and down to get in the necessary trim. His swinging arms looked rather formidable as they came in one of their movements within a couple of inches of Robson's chin.

'I'm going to change the order of diving,' Allerick said briskly. 'I've decided to put Collins first—to get the pull on Telford, who's bound to be first of Leigh's, I think. Then I'll come second.'

'And we have decided,' said Robson icily, without moving, 'that you will not come at all.'

'And what difference, may I ask, does your decision make to the swimming-captain?' Allerick answered, the wild glare springing into his eyes.

'This difference,' Robson replied, 'that you will leave the team.'

'I will *not* leave the team!'

'Oh yes, you will—yes, you will, Allerick,' Robson said firmly. 'We have no thieves in our——' He found himself in the water, gasping, with the feel of O'Shane's fist on his arrogant chin. 'And no bullies, either,' he continued, as he mounted the steps, looking calmly up at O'Shane. 'You can consider yourself chucked out of the team, O'Shane.'

'Chucked out? Why, I wouldn't touch

your filthy team with a ten-yard pole!
Look at them!' O'Shane retorted in a thick
expressive brogue, casting a contemptuous
hand towards the silent three. 'My hat!
Leigh's will laugh at you. The team can
leave the captain, which is what it amounts
to, but we stand more chance of winning
without you than you do without us.—Come
on, Rix, let's leave the fools!' O'Shane
rarely let himself go, but when he did he
was an impressive sight. The others did not
speak, and the three friends walked into the
dressing-room.

'Looks pretty hopeless now O'Shane's gone
as well,' Gregory ventured to remark. 'They
are the two best swimmers.'

'Rot!' snapped Robson briskly. 'We've
got to play up and let them see what we can
do. Now we've got to get two more in.—
Come on, Cairns, you don't swim half badly.—
Who else?'

'Spencer swims rather like an old boot,'
King said. 'We can't possibly put him in.'

'Well, we'll have to get one of the Fifth,
that's all.'

'Is it allowed?'

'Oh, I think so. It's just become a pre-
cedent to have the Sixth, that's all. Leigh's
don't always. D'Arcy was in the House-

team when he was in the Fifth. If they can do it, we can. Come on now, who can swim in the Fifth?'

'There's Slaney, who won the cup last year,' Gregory said. 'He'd give his eyes to go in the team.'

'Have a hunt for him before you strip, Cairns, old man,' ordered Robson. 'There's no time to be lost.'

Cairns went slowly away. He wasn't quite sure whether he wanted to be in the team under the new conditions, but it was too hot for anyone to think things out. Leigh's would win now in any case, so why worry?

But Allerick was thinking very deeply as he unfastened his bathing-costume. Suddenly he fastened it up again, and looked at O'Shane with glowing eyes. 'I say, Pat, don't dress!'

'Why? Got a wheeze?'

'Rather. Desmond's swimming-captain of Leigh's.'

'Yes.'

'Well, Desmond doesn't believe I pinched the medallion, does he?'

'I'm certain he doesn't, Rix. What's the big idea?'

'Well, which do you think he's likely to think most of—a team composed mostly of the Sixth, with Robson as leader, or a team composed mostly of the Fifth, with me as leader, and containing you and Whiskers?'

'Jove! Rix, I never thought of that. I don't know, I'm sure. But I can vouch for Desmond's belief in you, and Desmond is Leigh's captain. Let's try!'

'You forget,' Hare said, 'that perhaps you won't get three Fifth-form chaps to join you.'

'Pat will,' answered Allerick with perfect confidence. 'They'd lick his bally old boots. Oh, it's worth trying. Of course, don't let anything leak out to Robson and his gang.— Now, Pat, do your bestest.—Whiskers, get stripped.—Now, we'll stick our coats on and hike down to the junior baths. Pa Brown'll let us practice there if we tip him liberally.' He seemed to have taken fresh spirit.

O'Shane dressed himself enough to appear respectable in the School, and, slipping carefully out of the side door so that the four fellows in the water would not notice him, he ran across to the building and made for the Fifth-form common-room. The members of the Fifth were larking gaily, and crowded round him when he came in.

'Hullo, O'Shane!' cried Dale, the form-captain, an owlish-looking boy who was known among his comrades as 'Toots.' 'What have we done now?'

'I've secret business with you!' O'Shane said impressively. 'Let me see—where's Slaney?'

'Cairns came and landed him off to the swimming-baths a few minutes ago,' answered Dale. 'What's in the wind, O'Shane?'

'Hang it, they've grabbed the champion swimmer!' O'Shane growled. 'Which of you can swim?'

'Which can swim *fast*, do you mean?' Dale said. 'Well, here's the old Linnet——'

'Good — Lindsay, of course,' answered O'Shane. 'Who else?'

'I'm not such a bad shot at it myself,' Dale murmured bashfully. 'I dare say——'

'He can swim a lot steadier than Slaney,' piped Lindsay in the sweet soprano voice which had given him his nickname. 'Slaney's only brilliant at times, you know—when he's in the mood. I put my shilling on old Toots.'

'Well, that's fine. I want one more. Where's Black?'

'Hi, Smut!' called Dale, and a diminutive figure appeared from underneath the table.

Black, the joke of the Fifth form, was a fair, frail, blue-eyed boy who looked about eight rather than fifteen. He looked as if he would melt in water, but, as a matter of fact, he could swim like a fish. And also, he

thought the sun shone out of P. O'Shane.
'Do you want me?' he asked, looking eagerly
up out of his ridiculously wide eyes. 'I can
swim, O'Shane.'

For a moment O'Shane wondered if Leigh's
would raise a roar of derisive laughter at the
sight of tiny Black diving into the water
immediately after his own tall form. He
decided to risk it. After all, Hare was also
short; it wouldn't seem such a contrast. And
there was no room to think of trifles like size.
'Will you come into the team against
Leigh's?' he asked. 'Allerick's had to chuck
out three members of the team, so he's
decided to let the Fifth into it.'

'We're all for it!' cried Dale. 'But
where's Slaney gone to?'

'Oh, that's—er—another team,' O'Shane
answered hurriedly, brushing aside the awkward questions. 'Come on, you chaps, there's
no time to be lost.'

Allerick brightened visibly as he saw the
three youngsters slip into the cold water as
though it were their natural element. They
were in perfect condition, and entered into
the team-spirit immediately, obeying Allerick's
brisk orders without question.

'The worst of it is,' Allerick said, 'I'm
supposed to submit a list of the order in which

the team goes to Desmond in exchange for his. It's one of the conditions of the race. Now, supposing my team's questioned?'

'You jolly well get the list ready at once,' O'Shane said.

'Yes,' chimed in Hare; 'and give it to Desmond to-night.'

'I get you,' Allerick said. 'You mean Robson'll get his to Desmond first if we're not careful?'

'Rather.'

'Lend me your fountain-pen, Whiskers; I'll do it now,' Allerick said. 'I know the order. Those chaps are jolly good swimmers, aren't they?' he said, nodding towards the happy Fifth-formers, who were disporting themselves gaily at the far end of the baths, only too glad of an excuse for an extra lark in the water. He made the list out, and handed it to O'Shane.

'Hare, Black, Lindsay, Dale, O'Shane, Allerick,' read O'Shane aloud. 'What do I do with this, Rix?'

'Go and give it to Desmond,' Allerick answered, colouring a little.

'Not I! That's your job,' O'Shane said. 'See here, Rix, why not let bygones be bygones? Here's your chance.'

'Dash it!' Allerick answered furiously.

'How can I go and whine round him *now*? I don't like the fellow, and I don't like him any better because he's not inclined to think me a thief.'

'I hate to doubt you,' O'Shane said, 'but I can't help thinking that where Desmond is concerned, you're only obstinate. No, I won't take the list, and neither will Whiskers.— Will you?' he inquired, looking directly at Hare.

'No,' said Hare.

'Then I'll take it myself,' Allerick said. 'Well, I suppose I should, really.—Come on out, you fellows!' he called to the three others. 'How much longer are you going to mess there? And turn up prompt at three to-morrow afternoon. You know your places. You'll do fine. That's right!'

He gave the three a happy smile, and they decided that he couldn't possibly have pinched the medallion. But they ran to bring O'Shane things, gathered round him, and would, perhaps, have even fastened his shoes if he had let them.

Allerick's face, as he made his way across to Leigh's, wore an almost funereal expression. He did not want to speak to Desmond. He could not help remembering the last two interviews with the captain of Leigh's.

What if Desmond turned his list down contemptuously? Allerick shrugged his shoulders
to try to deceive himself into thinking he did
not care.

He met Lestrange in Leigh's passage.
Lestrange walked past him quickly, earnestly
studying the wall beyond Allerick. Allerick
smiled derisively. He glanced over the list
again before he knocked at the door of
Desmond's study. Everything inside was
very quiet. Allerick was glad he hadn't to
present the list to Desmond in the presence
of a crowd containing the laughing D'Arcy
or the fanatic Horton. And he could not
bear the thought of Sikes.

'Come in!' called Desmond. He was sitting on the floor, trying to fit together what
looked like parts of a bicycle. Somehow,
Allerick was taken aback at the sight of the
big fellow squatting there. Desmond looked
up, expecting it to be D'Arcy or Telford.
The quick colour ran up from his crumpled
soft collar to his rough brown hair. 'Oh,
hullo, Allerick,' he said, as though there were
no such things as inter-House feuds and lost
tempers and loosened teeth. 'I suppose you
couldn't tell me where this one goes?' He
held up a small piece of metal, and sat back on
his heels, looking up at Allerick and smiling.

'He's doing his noble-hero stunt,' thought Allerick. 'Forgiving and forgetting, like a character in *Eric, or Little by Little*.' He thrust the team-list ungraciously into Desmond's outstretched hand. 'Order of diving,' was his laconic explanation.

'Oh!' Desmond sprang to his feet, dropping the piece of metal that wouldn't fit. 'Thanks, Allerick.' He read the list. Allerick, watching intently, saw the expression of surprise which crossed his face. But all he said was, 'I see you're including some of the Fifth.' But he knew why, and when he saw Allerick was about to explain, he broke in with: 'I'll get mine, Allerick; I wasn't expecting you'd present yours before morning. Can you lend me a pen? Oh, here's one—let's see, I know—Lestrange, Desmond, Horton, Fendall, Telford, D'Arcy—that's right. There you are, Allerick. I hope it's a good match. Of course, we mean to beat you!'

'Maybe,' Allerick answered, as though unable to say more than one word at a time. He pocketed the list and walked to the door.

'Oh, don't go for a bit!' Desmond said. 'I've got some ripping lemonade!'

Allerick decided to clear the air and put things straight. It was one of those times

when he was about as tactful as a bull.
'Look here, Desmond,' he said, swinging
round to confront the other boy; 'are you
up to some game, or are you as thick-skinned
as a rhinoceros?'

Desmond winced as though he had been
struck, then he smiled at Allerick. It was
his last attempt, he knew, to win the captain
of Wright's. 'Neither,' he said; 'I'm just
persistent.'

'Wouldn't you think a jolly sight less of
me if I turned round and made up to you—
now, Desmond?'

'Oh, that—it just doesn't count with
me,' Desmond said. 'And the other'—he
touched his lip suggestively—'was just a
misunderstanding.'

Allerick hesitated for a moment, then he
knew he had no cause, except jealousy and
sheer mean-mindedness, to dislike Desmond.
'I'm jolly sorry,' he said with an effort.
'Will you——'

Desmond's hand shot out immediately.
'Oh, this is awfully decent!' he said. 'Now
between us we'll put an end to this beastly
quarrel——'

Allerick frowned a little, remembering the
evening in his own study when plans for the
end of the quarrel had gone forward. But

he thrust the recollection from him. 'So that was your game,' he laughed a little bitterly. 'And nothing else—it's part of your peace idea to get pally with me, of course.'

Desmond kicked the pieces of metal under the table, and looked round again, rubbing his firm chin thoughtfully. 'Not exactly, Rix,' he said; 'I was considering another thing too.'

'Oh—what?' inquired Allerick, deciding that the matter would have to be straightened before Desmond and he were on a friendly footing.

'But perhaps you object to being called a thing!' Desmond went on, turning to the cupboard. 'I say, you will have some of this topping lemonade, won't you, old man?'

Allerick smiled at last, and sat down as one taking possession. 'Well, I don't mind if I do—er—Des,' he answered.

CHAPTER X.

THE SWIMMING MATCH.

WHEN Allerick had gone, Desmond dashed into the next study as fast as his long legs would carry him. D'Arcy and Telford were having a sparring game, and the room was rather untidy.

'Good gracious, look at old Des!' cried Telford, brushing his hair away from his damp forehead.

'Been left a fortune, old man?' inquired D'Arcy. 'Or don't you feel well?'

Desmond flushed brilliantly, but his smile continued. 'Guess who's been jawing to me?'

'Rix!' cried Telford at once, as the most unlikely person.

'How did you guess?'

'Dunno. Well, tell us! What did he want?'

'Brought his team-list—here—and was off away as huffy as you like and—er—I don't know how it happened, but—well, he's ever so pally. Isn't it fine?—I say, Darkie, we must find out who pinched the medallion. Rix is awfully decent; really, it's rotten for a chap like him to be accused.'

'I'm sure if you once turn your mighty brain upon the affair it will clear up!' laughed D'Arcy. 'But does this prodigal-son business with old Rix mean we'll be getting on friendly terms with Wright's?'

'I hope so, old man,' answered Desmond enthusiastically.

D'Arcy sighed deeply and theatrically. 'I was just going to buy a twopenny note-book to put down my plans for rags,' he groaned. 'But there's still time. Rix doesn't represent Wright's at present.'

'Darkie, don't be a rotter!' Telford said.— 'I say, though, Desmond, Allerick's put some of the Fifth in this list.'

'I reckon the Sixth have left the team,' Desmond said. 'But it's still a fair fight. The Smut, for instance, is a tophole swimmer.'

'Did you give Allerick some of my lemonade?' questioned D'Arcy suddenly.

'I say, you suspicious blighter!' Desmond said. 'Upon my word——'

'Did you?'

'Now, I ask you, Darkie, is it the kind of thing——'

'Here, Tiger, let's go and have a look at

that lemonade !' suggested D'Arcy, and they all went back to the other study.

Hardly had they got in when a knock came at the door and Robson entered. His smile was particularly patronising and supercilious. He glanced at the untidy pair of boxers with contempt and handed Desmond a sheet of note-paper. His way of handing it was peculiar too ; he held it up on a level with Desmond's face, and when Leigh's captain took it, stood with one hand on his hip in a most self-satisfied manner.

Desmond was mystified at first when he saw that list ; but a second later he understood. Not by a flicker did his expression change—he looked at Robson in cold surprise. 'What, may I ask, is this ?' inquired he.

' That,' answered Robson, speaking slowly and distinctly, as though Desmond were a very small child, 'is the order of diving for Wright's team in the swimming contest to-morrow.'

'Oh ! And since when have you been Wright's swimming-captain ?' questioned Desmond.

' Oh, that's all right !' laughed Robson airily, though a nasty little gleam lit his eyes for a second at Desmond's tone. 'We've decided Allerick's not suitable for the position, so——'

' Very interesting,' cut in Desmond, and his blue eyes spoke volumes ; 'but it happens that I already have the order of diving from the official swimming - captain of Wright's, whose name is Allerick. Perhaps, since you are so ignorant on the point, he would not mind you seeing it. Here . . .' He picked up Allerick's list from the table and handed it to Robson. The Tiger raised his hand to his mouth to conceal a smile. D'Arcy didn't bother to conceal his. But Desmond was not smiling; he could not have said whether it was dislike of Robson's curved lip, or defence of Allerick which drove him, but he wanted beyond anything just then to make Robson feel small. And he did.

'What's this?' inquired Robson, flicking Allerick's paper almost at Desmond's nose. 'He can't—you won't——' He was furious. Gone was the insolent, contemptuous smile, the arrogant bearing.

'I have already told you what that is. This is what has to be explained,' and Desmond handed back Robson's list.

Robson threw it down on the floor and almost stamped on it. He was white to the lips. 'You senseless idiot!' he said. 'Do you think you can treat me like this and get off with it? But I might have known a gutter-snipe like you would uphold a thief like Allerick. I——' He found himself looking

at Desmond's big clenched fist. Above it
was Desmond's blazing blue eyes, which he,
even the great Robson, could not confront.

'Take care,' warned Desmond; 'no one
insults Allerick to me.'

'You'll find your mistake,' Robson fumed,
backing to the door. 'Allerick 'll be chucked
out yet, and then I'll start on you. Wait,
that's all.' The door slammed behind him.
D'Arcy laughed uproariously.

'Perhaps it would have been better if
you'd just handed back his list and left it at
that,' Telford said thoughtfully. 'Robson's
not the kind of chap *I*'d like to offend.
No.'

Desmond was very thoughtful. 'What the
Aunt Kate did he mean,' questioned he, 'by
saying that Allerick'd be chucked out, and
then he'd start on me? Sounded as though
he . . .' He broke off, and then went on again
as though enlightened. 'Is it the fact that
Robson led the gang who searched Rix's
study and found the medallion?'

'It is, Sherlock,' answered D'Arcy, gazing
dolefully at the empty lemonade-siphon. 'At
least, that's how all the accounts go. I think
you're a dirty, big, greedy, guzzling hound,
N. Desmond. I sha'n't let you play with my
jacksharps any more.'

Desmond took no notice. He was gazing out of the window as though he had never seen that particular part of the tennis-courts before.

'Oho, Holmes is concentrating on the blood-stains,' D'Arcy breathed dramatically to the Tiger. 'He has a clue! Ha-ha, it comes—the deduction!' For Desmond had rubbed his head furiously and blinked.

'Penny for them,' said the Tiger.

'Oh no; it's too rotten. Nobody'd do it,' murmured Desmond irrelevantly. 'I say, we must do something to help him solve that mystery.'

'I think you said that before, old son,' answered D'Arcy. 'Let's feed.'

'I'm going to bed early,' said Desmond, 'and so're you, Darkie and Tiger. We've got to win that match to-morrow.'

.   .   .   .   .   .

Never, Desmond decided, had there been such a lovely day as dawned that Saturday. Rain fell during the night, and the air in the morning was so cool and sweet that O'Shane, leaning far out of the little window of the cubicle, exclaimed loudly, 'It smells like Coleraine.'

'I never felt more like a swimming contest in my life!' declared Desmond to D'Arcy, through the cubicle wall.

'Let's see what it looks like!' D'Arcy laughed, and sprang upon the bed to look over the wooden division.

Desmond was towelling his glowing face, and blinked up at his friend happily. 'What a pity we don't have open-air baths,' he said; 'it's so jolly sunny.'

'The sun puts me off my stroke,' D'Arcy said. 'Oh, I could swim to America! Wright's haven't a chance.'

'Perhaps Rix feels the same.'

'It's a good job such a feat is impossible, then. What's America done?'

'Shame, Darkie! A chap can't help his looks.'

'It's easy for some people to talk,' answered D'Arcy, springing to ground again. Desmond glanced quickly in his mirror and reddened with happy conceit.

It was rather hard to keep the members of the team from eating a heavy breakfast, the crisp air made for huge appetites, but Desmond achieved it by sitting at the head of the Sixth-form table and talking loudly about boiled pork and dog-biscuits.

Morning school was excused because of the match, which was planned for eleven, so all they had to do was to walk round the field and talk excitedly.

'There's one weak point in Allerick's team,' said Desmond, 'and that's Hare. Hare's a good swimmer, but he's not fast. Rix had to put him in. I wish it was the old team; I'd feel somehow it was a bigger fight. But it's quite fair. It's perfectly fair.'

'You could have accepted Robson's list,' D'Arcy suggested, his eyes twinkling, then he dodged to escape Desmond's answering box of the ears.—''Lo, Tiger! How do you feel?'

'Fit!' answered the Tiger, sauntering lazily up, hands in pockets. 'What time is it?'

'Ten-thirty. Perhaps we'd better go and get ready. Where's Lestrange? Must give him a last few tips.'

Lestrange arrived, looking so like frail china that one would have thought, as of Black, that water would be the last thing he could face. But Desmond surveyed him with contentment.

'Good man, Les,' he approved; 'you'll get a fair start, and I'll keep it.—Hor, come here; you must dive straight, and don't be in too much of a hurry, you know. Forget it's a match against Wright's, and imagine you're a Scotch terrier chasing a five-pound

note that the wind's blowing.—And Fendall,
don't splash—the spectators come to watch,
not to receive their annual. Pa Leigh hasn't
yet forgotten the time you wet his glasses.—
And Tiger, I've nothing to say to you.
You're the big gun. And Darkie finishes
up. I'm chancing on Darkie not fluking . . .'
He turned and gave D'Arcy a tremendous
thump on the back. 'Come on! The baths
are getting full already.'

They made for the big double door.
Wright's team were drinking half-glasses of
lemonade, while Allerick gave his final
warnings to them. Robson was standing
near at hand, and Desmond saw him pass
Black's glass to him and smile as though he
were on the best terms with all the world.
He was clad in white flannels and the very
last thing in blazers, and only when he saw
Desmond did the wicked gleam flash from
his eyes one moment and subside. Desmond
saw him smiling and debonair, and distrusted
his joviality more than his fury. But he did
not let Robson see that he had noticed him.
Turning to Allerick, he smiled and said,
'Everything square?'

'Rather,' agreed Allerick, with a strange
mixture of rough shyness and reluctant
admiration in his face. 'Want some lemon?'

'Ten-to. Yes, I think we might,' answered Desmond, calling his team up, and they drank the bitter stuff as they undressed. At five to eleven the two teams walked leisurely out to the spring-boards, and the spectators cheered wildly for whichever team had their support. Mr Brown, the swimming-instructor, fastened a red cord to the bar beneath the board, for each boy to touch as he returned, his follower not being allowed to dive until he had done this.

At the judges' desk sat the Head-master and Mr Clare, the games-master. Mr Brown fired the pistol, and the leaders dived. Lestrange came swiftly and gracefully as though it were but a pleasure to him. Hare was concentrating in an agony of anxiety; but he did his best, and though he finished up more than two arm-lengths behind Lestrange, Allerick smiled as Black sprang two or three seconds after Desmond's mighty form took the water in a supremely lovely curve. The Smut's tiny body was such a contrast to that of the captain of Leigh's that the spectators started a laugh, and there were more cries of 'Go it, Smut!' than of 'Keep it, Des!' But the Smut gained. Tiny as his white little arms and legs were in comparison with the muscular Viking limbs of Desmond, he gained—for he swam like some little sea creature, with astonishing rapidity.

Then something happened. The cheering died. Desmond went ahead, but the easy motion of the Smut's legs stopped abruptly, his arms beat the water feebly for a moment or two to no purpose; then they, too, ceased, his blue eyes closed, and his round little curl-clad head went under the pale-green water.

The spectators did not grasp matters at first, and Desmond had reached the far end of the baths before the shout rose, 'The Smut's ill.'

Mr Brown ran forward, and Allerick dived like a flash into the water, but someone was before him. Robson's expensive blazer lay on the edge of the swimming-pool, and he was in the water, had dived and seized the small limp form of the Smut before anyone had grasped his action. He laid the Smut on the marble tiles and, kneeling down beside him, started to rub the boy's legs. Mr Brown rushed forward; and Desmond, hearing with astonishment the cries, 'Well done, Robson!' climbed out of the water and came forward.

Robson stood up again. His beautiful

white trousers clung dripping round his legs, his shining hair fell over his grey eyes. They cheered him, and he looked down at the poor little Smut as he lay there, and he met Desmond's astonished blue eyes. Yes, it was a quick and a brave thing, thought Desmond; yet why, when Robson stood there, apparently so unconcerned at the cheering, so depreciative of what he had done—why should he dislike him more than he had done last night?

'What's up?' asked Desmond, bending over the Fifth-former.

'Can't think,' said Mr Brown. 'I've sent for Dr Gray. It isn't cramp; it seems as if he just fainted, and yet it was so sudden. His heart's all right; it's almost as if he's been drugged or something. The doctor'll know. Just help me to lift him into the dressing-room, Desmond.—You come, too, Robson; you must get those things off.'

Desmond lifted the little boy up and, laying him on the bench in the dressing-room, started to pull off his costume. Robson gave a last glance at the two, and went out again—to be greeted by more cheers, which he ignored in the same manner.

'I'll go and get hot towels or something to put on him. Put this round him, Des-

mond, and keep on rubbing him,' ordered
Mr Brown. 'Ah, here's Allerick.—Don't let
anyone else come in here, Allerick. Help
Desmond. I'll be back in a minute.'

Allerick, clad in a multi-coloured dressing-
gown, looked particularly hideous, but there
was anxiety in his brown eyes. 'Poor old
Smut,' he said, picking up one of Black's
arms to chafe. 'Cramp, I suppose?'

'No,' answered Desmond, looking up and
frowning, 'it isn't cramp.'

'Oh, what is it, then?'

'Brown doesn't know, but the doc will.
Brown said it was almost—as—if he'd been
drugged.'

'Rot! Rot!' Allerick's face whitened.
'Does he mean foul play?'

'Looks like it, Rix,' Desmond said. 'But
who'd drug the little beast? I say, he's
coming to!'

Black had certainly stirred. His eyelids
fluttered, then he opened his eyes. He looked
almost pathetically young and small.

'Hullo, old son! How d'you feel?' asked
Desmond, smiling down at him.

The Smut's lips moved, but he made no
audible answer.

At that moment Dr Gray appeared.
'What's this? What's this? Dear me!'

he murmured. He was a fussy little man, who kept up an aimless stream of talk while he worked. He bent over Black, sounding his heart, raising his eyelid, then he poured something between the pale parted lips. 'The boy's been drugged!' he said. 'Just before entering the water, I should say. Poor little chap! What a school this is!'

Mr Brown slipped quickly to the door, and closed it firmly. 'Drugged, did you say? Well, don't shout it out.—Not a word, Desmond and Allerick. You understand? We don't want any more mistakes. The School doesn't seem to hold a certificate of good conduct at present.'

'Who on earth'd benefit by drugging him?' Desmond questioned, then suddenly the colour rushed over his face. Had Allerick seen? But Allerick was still looking down at the little boy. Desmond called himself a rotter for even entertaining for a moment the thought that it would be to Allerick's benefit to drug the Smut. To cover over his feelings he asked Allerick, 'What about the match, Rix? Shall we carry on with the other four, or postpone it?'

'Postpone it,' answered Allerick at once. 'There can't be any match to-day.'

'As you like,' Desmond said. 'Well, anyway, half the chaps have gone now. Upon my word, you never know what's going to happen next! Everything was so ripping.' He sighed and suddenly shivered, realising his unclad condition.

'This certainly isn't the kind of thing you'd expect to happen,' Allerick said bitterly. 'What's St Martin's coming to? Thieves and match-foulers!'

'It's rotten,' Desmond agreed. 'Let's go and dress, old son. Here's another beastly mystery to solve now.'

'Perhaps the School'll bring it home to the same fellow as the other one,' said Allerick, as though he didn't care a button if they did.

But Desmond stopped suddenly, his blue eyes blazing. 'Rix, what a thing to say! They couldn't!'

'There were a lot of things I thought they couldn't do at one time,' answered Allerick with hard directness; 'but I'm older and wiser now. And, as Pat O'Shane says,' he added with a sudden burst of fierceness, '"I'll fight while I've got a shred of shirt left."'

'That's more the way to talk!' Desmond said approvingly. 'Don't think nasty things, Rix, when they might never happen. You're getting cynical.'

'It's easy for some people to talk!' snapped Allerick, in the very words D'Arcy had used that morning.

But Desmond did not redden this time. 'You can't insult me, Rix,' he said. 'I'm playing Pat O'Shane's trump card now—persistence.'

CHAPTER XI.

ALLERICK RESIGNS.

BUT it is wonderful how things leak out, and at a public school, once a rumour is started, there is no power on earth can keep it from spreading. So soon there came a whisper that the Smut had been drugged. Desmond told no one, and Allerick told no one, and Mr Brown told only Dr Newton. But both boys, at least, remembered that Robson had been standing by when Mr Brown gave it as his opinion that Black's condition had been due to a drug.

Robson, then, was responsible for the thing getting round. But who started the whispering that Allerick's team had been very poor, that his best swimmers had resigned, that he had put the Fifth in, that he did not want the match to take place, and so on and so on, from evil conclusion to evil conclusion?

Poor Allerick! No wonder he began to think an evil fate was pursuing his every move. No wonder his temper grew more frayed every day. He, who had never known

what fear was, was getting nervous. He was
not guilty, yet he feared to meet the eyes of
the others. He was afraid to go round the
School alone, yet he snapped at O'Shane whenever the Irishman spoke to him. Allerick was
not blessed with a martyr's patience nor the
gift of firm endurance. He covered his misery
with rough bitterness, and when he was most
angry he shut himself up in his study, and
sat at the table, glaring at the ink-stains on
its surface until he knew their positions off
by heart.

And meanwhile Robson acted the retiring
hero, and made himself popular in Wright's
by a lavish expenditure on tuck and entertain-
ment. The more Allerick withdrew, the more
Robson came forward. In the final Inter-
School Shield match against Dale's he made
seventy-eight, and was cheered and cheered
again, and for some time took Desmond's
place as St Martin's great cricketer; for something at the match made Desmond nervous
and his play was below its usual standard.

Desmond was worried. True, the feud
between Leigh's and Wright's had died away
to an almost incredible extent, but it was not
because the captains of the Houses had become
friends, as Desmond had once so sanguinely
desired. It was rather because Wright's was

too busy with its own affairs to bother with Leigh's. Allerick was defied and disobeyed. Only the Fifth form attempted to do anything he ordered, and that was only because O'Shane endorsed his every command. Things began to grow desperate.

'You've only one thing to do,' Hare suggested, 'report them to the Newt. He told you to go to him if things got stiff, didn't he?'

'How can I report prefects like Cairns or Gregory?' asked Allerick. His face was pale and there were shadows of sleeplessness under his eyes.

'Why not, when they've offended like the others?'

'I won't!' declared Allerick. 'I will not make Wright's a laughing-stock for the whole School. I'm going to resign.'

'Oh, Rix!' Hare said. 'That's not like you.' Then he noticed Allerick's bent head and tired mouth. 'Unless you're groggy,' he said very slowly, his grey eyes serious.

'You've hit it,' said Allerick, too weary to protest or lose his temper; 'I am.'

O'Shane came in at this moment, and felt the heavy atmosphere as soon as he entered. 'Now, what's up?' asked he.

'Rix is talking of resigning,' Hare said,

'that's all.' He expected O'Shane to raise a loud outcry, but all the Irishman did was to cross to the window and gaze thoughtfully out.

'I've been talking to Des,' the latter said, turning round suddenly.

'No wonder you look queer!' snapped Allerick.

'You're irrelevant, Pat!' smiled Hare.

'Not so much as you think. I can't repeat all Desmond said, because we had a rather private conversation . . .'

Allerick's mouth twisted a little. Truly, he was getting suspicious of his best friends. He wished suddenly he were anywhere but at St Martin's.

'Desmond,' said O'Shane, 'is a jolly clever chap——'

'Really?' came a gruff voice from outside the window, and like the fabulous camel's, Desmond's head and shoulders appeared through the window. 'May I come in?' he asked. 'I'm so glad I'm a jolly clever chap, Pat.'

'Jolly clever to come up just at that moment,' O'Shane laughed. 'Busts the theory that listeners never hear any good of themselves. But I was just telling Rix that you've got a sort of clue, Des.'

'I hope you didn't——'

'No, I didn't tell Rix all you said; knew you wouldn't want me to. I just told him you were going on the lines of giving a rogue a rope to hang himself.'

'That's so,' said Desmond. 'But, I say, Rix, don't think I've got much to work on. It's just a sort of feeling in my bones, and they don't carry much weight, these feelings.'

'Don't be so sure, Desmond,' Hare broke in. 'Do you know, I'm inclined to think sometimes they carry more weight than some chaps' cut-and-dried conclusions?'

Allerick gave him a swift appreciative glance before he turned to Desmond and said, 'Well, anyway, what's this got to do with my resigning the captaincy?'

'Were you seriously thinking of resigning the captaincy?' asked Desmond.

'Yes,' said Allerick.

'Why?'

'Oh, one reason and another,' Allerick muttered vaguely, because he wasn't going to let any member of Leigh's, even Desmond, know the trouble Wright's were giving him.

'Perhaps you'd do just as well to resign,' Desmond said. 'Not that you're not the best chap for the job, but I've a kind of idea you'd get your position back quicker if you did——'

'The captaincy is the rope,' O'Shane put in.

'Shut up, Pat!' ordered Desmond. 'I'm not letting myself in for any statements. Allerick knows I wouldn't advise him to quit without good reason, I bet. He knows he can trust me.—Don't you, Allerick?'

He received no answer, and thinking that Allerick intended none, the colour rushed into his cheeks and he made a little stiff movement forward. Both Hare and O'Shane noticed it.

But Hare noticed also that Allerick was deep in his own thoughts and his eyes had a far-away look. He shook Allerick's shoulder. 'Here, wake up, Rix!' he said. 'Des asked you a question.'

Allerick straightened and looked round at Desmond. 'Eh?' he said vaguely. 'What were you saying? Sorry.'

'I—er—forget,' Desmond murmured.

But O'Shane said, 'Desmond just said he knew you could trust him, didn't he?'

'Why did he make a question out of it?' asked Allerick, and smiled, and somehow Desmond thought the rough sentence was the best thing he had ever heard.

'You shouldn't go to sleep in the middle

of my most important perorations, Rix,' said he, with a little laugh.

'You advised me to quit the captaincy, didn't you?'

'Yes, I did.'

'Then I will,' Allerick decided suddenly. 'Not altogether because you advised me, of course—don't get conceited enough to think that—but nobody seems to jump at me as a traitor now when I talk of resigning. Better to have a captain the chaps want, whether he's a thief or not, than an unpopular fellow. —What says Whiskers?'

'Do whatever you like,' Hare answered doubtfully.

'Whiskers doesn't want me to resign.'

'Oh, Desmond knows best, of course,' Hare said. 'I'm prejudiced by House feeling, as you might say—he isn't. But who'll be captain if you resign, Rix?'

'That's just the point,' Desmond interrupted eagerly. 'If a captain resigns in midterm without stating adequate reason, his successor is appointed by vote of the House.'

'Is he? By Jove! how you *do* swot the rules up,' Allerick answered. 'But do you think the Head'll stick to that rule? I don't think it's ever been applied before.'

'It's never had to be,' retorted Desmond.

'Oh, the Newt 'll stick to it all right. And then—we 'll see——'

'Or we won't see,' Hare said.

'Oh, I think we will!' Desmond cried cheerfully.—'Keep your pecker up, Rix! As D'Arcy says every time he breaks a rule and doesn't get caught: "Innocence is its own defence."'

'That 's just rot!' Allerick said.

'Perhaps not in the long run,' was Desmond's parting shot. 'So long, then; I 'll see you in the morning!' He vaulted lightly through the window and disappeared.

'Desmond 's got something up his sleeve,' Hare said, 'and I think I 've an idea what he means. But what will the Newt say when you resign, Rix?'

'I 'll tell you when I 've been,' answered Allerick. 'I 'll go first thing in the morning. There 's nothing particular to attend to, so it 's a good time to resign. It doesn't look as if we 'll manage to fix the swimming contest up. The Smut isn't keen on swimming now, although he 's recovered, and Des never mentions the affair. Suppose he thinks it 's too painful. Yes, I 'll resign.'

'Sleep on it, and do whatever 's your waking decision,' advised Hare in his gravest tones.

But Allerick's morning decision was that

of the night before.　At any rate, he would
go to Dr Newton and ask to resign.　One
had to put the interest of the House first.
He was very serious as he made his way to
the Head-master's study, but again he felt
a glow of new confidence at the sight of
Dr Newton clad in unscholarly flannels and
standing by the open window to read his
paper.

It was a sign of the Doctor's youth that he
was at his best in the morning.　He smiled
when he saw Allerick.　'Good-morning,' he
said.　'Isn't it a beautiful day?　Makes one
feel glad to be alive.　What can I do for
you, Allerick?'

'I—er—I would like to resign the captaincy
of Wright's, sir,' Allerick answered in a low
voice.

The Head-master threw his paper upon
the table and motioned Allerick to sit down.
'What made you decide to resign?' he
questioned.　'Have things become *too* difficult?　I asked you to come and tell me how
affairs went on, you know,' he added, with
a reproachful smile.

'I *could* continue to be captain,' answered
Allerick; 'but—I think it would be better
for the House if I resigned.'

'Are you sure, though, Allerick?　Have

you thought it well over? You know, if you resign now, the new captain will be chosen by a general vote?'

'Yes, sir.'

'And you think the House is capable of choosing an efficient captain?'

Allerick hesitated. He did not know what to say. He could not tell the Head that he felt depressed and nervous, or that Desmond had advised him to resign. They both sounded such feeble excuses. He was relieved when the Head went on, without forcing him to answer.

'Well, Allerick, I won't make things any harder for you than they are. I'll accept your resignation without further question. And don't worry, boy; don't worry. You look worn out. If you only knew it, you're very lucky—discovering who are your friends. And I notice there isn't so much friction between Wright's and Leigh's Houses. Sweet are the uses of adversity. Very well, Allerick, you resign; but I'll reserve the right to return you at the end of the term, and make the new captain temporary.'

'Oh, thank you, sir,' Allerick said, straightening his shoulders with new confidence, and he rose to go.

'No, stay here, Allerick,' said the Head. 'Won't you have breakfast with me?'

He rang the bell and, when Seddon appeared, ordered a breakfast for two that revived Allerick's appetite wonderfully. There was something soothing in the atmosphere of the room too, in the scent of the flowers nodding about the window, and the vivid sunshine falling across the Head-master's hair and the silver dishes on the table, to form a square of silver on the grey carpet. Allerick felt marvellously cheered and strengthened. Wright's, and all its cares, seemed a thousand miles away while the Head chatted about cricket and Switzerland and the yacht race and the Geneva conference and a score of other things. Once he said 'ripping,' and then caught himself up and looked sharply at Allerick to see if the boy had noticed ; then he went on chatting and said 'topping' without even noticing. And Allerick liked him more and more all the time, and was sorry when the chapel-bell went and he had to take his departure.

After prayers Dr Newton announced coldly that the captain of Wright's House, Allerick, had resigned, and the new captain would be chosen that afternoon by ballot of the House, at which Mr Wright would preside. Nominations were to be handed in to Mr Wright during the day. He himself had nothing to do with it, he added, and gave the ranks of Wright's a long scrutiny, which caused some of their members to colour uncomfortably.

There was not much attention paid to lessons that morning. At eleven, when they went for milk and biscuits, there was one name on the black-board in the class-room— 'O'Shane.' A few minutes later it was gone; Mr Wright had erased it at the Irishman's infuriated bidding. In its place came at lunch-time the name 'Robson,' and later King and Cairns were proposed. No one seemed to add to these three. To Allerick the result was patent. He met Desmond outside after the afternoon school.

'Aren't you going to the ballot, Rix?' asked Desmond. 'Who's nominated?'

Allerick told him.

'What's the use of voting?' he asked. 'Robson's as good as got it. Anyway, I couldn't bring myself to vote for King or Cairns.'

'But—Robson . . .' Desmond said. 'It's Robson you want to vote for.'

'Robson!'

'Yes, of course, he's got to be captain. It would be awful if anyone else got in. Oh, you're awfully thick, Rix!' cried Desmond, laughing. 'Don't look so astounded. I love

Robbie about as much as you do; but, don't
you see, he's got to be given the rope!'

'The — rope?   Do   you   mean   to   say
you——'

''S-sh—not so loud—walls have ears. There's
Darkie.—Darkie!   Coo-ee!'

'Hullo!'   Darkie   came   running   towards
them.   'Hullo,   Rix,   whatever   made   you
resign?   There's the little tin-pot millionaire
got in now.'

'Is that a fact?' asked Desmond, looking
very relieved.

'Rather.   He seems to be the big pot of
Wright's at present.   Cairns only got two
votes, and——'

'Robson got all the rest,' O'Shane added,
appearing as if by magic between them.
'Well, Desmond, are you satisfied?'

'Quite,' said Desmond.

'I'd love to know what you are up to,'
D'Arcy said.   'Des   sat   glowering   at   the
coffee all brekker, and it was quite decent
coffee, too.   You wouldn't believe how queer
he looks when he's thinking.   It's a good
job he doesn't often do it.   Why all this
sudden affection for Robson?'

'It would be awful if we were mistaken,
Pat!' said Desmond, suddenly turning to
O'Shane.

'We can but wait and see,' O'Shane answered. 'It's no use sitting back and doing nothing. And I don't think we *are* mistaken. Look!'

Robson was coming out of the door of Wright's House in the midst of an excited throng, who were patting his back and shaking his hands and cheering gaily. He was glowing with pride when he caught sight of Allerick standing with the other three there. Desmond, quick at reading expressions, guessed that Wright's new captain was wishing Allerick was standing lonely there—it would have been such a triumph then. But Allerick was in the company of the captain of Leigh's, and Leigh's football-captain, and O'Shane—and somehow these three seemed to make a more effective bodyguard than all the cheering crowd around Robson himself.

Robson suddenly shook his congratulators away and with a few swift strides reached the four boys. He did not speak, but he looked first Allerick and then Desmond from head to foot with glinting mockery in his grey eyes.

Desmond laughed. 'Congratulations, Robson,' said he. 'It must be good to be so popular.'

Robson became apparently perfectly friendly, ignoring all the group except Desmond.

'Thank you, Desmond,' he said quietly. 'I'm glad you're so decent over it. I thought perhaps . . . But never mind, now we can work together for the general good of both our Houses, eh?' He held out his hand.

Desmond moved his own right hand as though to take Robson's, then suddenly he converted the action, and slipped it through Allerick's arm. He enjoyed seeing the smile freeze on Robson's face, and his hand drop to his side again. 'I am working *now* for the general good of both the Houses,' he said, and turning round, Allerick and he went off arm in arm.

D'Arcy looked round at Robson and laughed. 'Your crowd's getting impatient!' he said. 'Aren't you going to celebrate? It must be good to be so popular.'

Robson bit his lip furiously. 'Desmond is a fool.'

'You can repeat that if you want to go to your blow-out with two black eyes,' D'Arcy answered sweetly.

Robson went back to his crowd of supporters, the pleasant, almost shy smile returning to his handsome face as he did so.

CHAPTER XII.

'MACBETH.'

AT any rate, Robson appeared to be very popular. With the exception of the three Sixth-formers and the members of the Fifth form who followed O'Shane in all things, Wright's flocked round him and made him much more of a power than Allerick had ever been.

Desmond began to wonder if he had done right in advising Allerick to resign. But though he frequently acted on impulse, in this case he had thought the matter out with an unusual amount of care. What he had not meant to do was to let Robson see his dislike of him. In the first place, it would hinder his plan—a solution of the mystery of Allerick's treatment; and in the second place, he knew he would stand no chance of healing the breach between the two Houses if he refused Robson's so-called friendship. But his open generous nature had revolted at the thought of taking Robson's hand, especially in Allerick's presence. Of

course, he could not do it. He had been
tactless in his refusal, and as good as told
Robson to do his worst. And Robson did.
Carefully, it is true, but surely. He dropped
hints here and there, and suggested rags to
play on Leigh's. He had no need to
suggest their execution. Gregory and King
took him at his slightest hint. Then the
juniors were incited, carefully too, and
Leigh's juniors retaliated hotly, and hardly
a day went by without a skirmish between
the two crowds of boys. Desmond did all
he could to prevent Leigh's from paying
Wright's back, but he could only control a
certain section of Leigh's, and while he was
keeping one form in order, another was
playing a wicked prank. Truly, the days
became exciting, one never knew what
would happen next. Desmond hoped Dr
Newton would command Robson to stop
the feud, but Robson was so clever that he
never appeared to be implicated in any of
the affairs, but rather to be very hard on
the offenders.

One night, about a fortnight after Robson's
appointment, Desmond was taking his usual
evening stroll round the field with D'Arcy
and Telford. 'I'm glad you're behaving
yourself, Darkie,' he said. 'I don't know

what I'd do if you were acting like you did in Ranger's time.'

'It's not my fault I'm not,' said D'Arcy mournfully. 'I'd be only too glad to have a few knocks at Wright's. I'm tired of being kept in order. But anything to oblige.'

Desmond gave him an affectionate dig in the ribs. 'You're in with us to the death, you ass. Robson'll be only rattier than ever if he can't get us ratty. He's deep, too.'

'I've a kind of instinct against Robson, somehow,' the Tiger murmured. 'I don't know why.'

'I guess I do,' D'Arcy said. 'I've more than an instinct against him.'

Desmond was about to speak again when McLaren joined them and interrupted the conversation. 'Have you decided about the play?' he asked.

'What play?' asked Desmond.

'You know, we were wondering whether to act *Macbeth* before the School or not. Proceeds to go with the subs to the new wing of the Ranley Hospital.'

'We seem to pretty well be building that new wing for them,' Desmond growled. 'The School House had a concert, then there was the subscription list, and now a play.'

'It was the idea of Leigh's doing something special that made us think of *Macbeth*,' McLaren said. 'We know the play so well already. We could get all the big parts out of the Sixth, and give the minor ones to a few of the Fifth. It wouldn't be much trouble, and it would be such a lark. Besides, we might be excused a few lessons to rehearse.'

'Calculating mind of the Scot!' Desmond laughed. 'Anything to get out of work! Well, have the play by all means, but don't expect me to take part, unless it's one where there's no spouting.'

'But Lestrange said you'd play Macbeth,' McLaren persisted.

'Me play Macbeth? Great Scott!' cried Desmond. 'Catch me!'

'He can't say two words before an audience without stuttering,' put in Telford.

Desmond's vanity was piqued at once. 'What's that?' he snapped. 'I bet I could take the part if I liked.'

'Oh, you could do wonders!' laughed the Tiger. 'I can imagine you, old bean'—he threw out his arm and recited, with a good imitation of Desmond's gruff tones—'S-s-so f-f-foul and f-fair a-a d-day I have n-n-not s-s-s-s-seen!'

'Oh well, it's all off, then,' McLaren said. 'I don't think Lestrange knew what your elocution was like. He said you were the biggest chap in the School; and I said, ay, you'd look bonny in a kilt; and so he said, "Let Des be Macbeth, then." That's all. But since you——'

'But I will play Macbeth!' Desmond said, crimsoning. 'I can if I want. I d-d-don't s-stutter at all.'

'Oh n-n-no,' mimicked D'Arcy. 'When you're calm you speak all right. But how about being on the stage before all the School and the Staff?'

'It won't make any difference if I get my part off properly.'

'Oh, but it will!' D'Arcy said.

'It won't. I only stammered in the German play last year because I couldn't remember my part and it was a foreign language. Look here . . .' He went off into the dagger speech, looking with great ferocity at McLaren and pronouncing every word clearly, without stammering once.

McLaren applauded loudly, but D'Arcy and Telford shook their heads and laughed.

'I dare say he'll do as well as anyone else, though,' said the Tiger, 'unless it's Lestrange, and I suppose he's going to be Lady Macbeth.'

'He is,' answered McLaren. 'And I'm Banquo; and he wants you to be Malcolm, and D'Arcy, Macduff. Then Horton's to be Duncan, and Fendall's Donalbain; then Waugh is Ross. Of course, Palmer won't take a part—the talking would be too fatiguing, I suppose; and Sikes hasn't made up his mind yet whether he'll be Lady Macduff or the porter. Young Sefton is going to be the first witch, and we haven't picked the others yet. But don't you think it's a good idea?'

'Rather!' said Telford enthusiastically. 'I love showing off. I wish he'd given me a bigger part than Malcolm.—Let *me* be Macbeth, Desmond!'

'Not likely!' responded Desmond, now thoroughly obstinate about his histrionic powers which he had just discovered. 'It's only fitting the captain of the House should play the title-rôle.'

'Then I hope you make a mess of it!' the Tiger retorted.

'Naughty, naughty,' reprimanded Desmond. 'Don't be vindictive, Tiger.'

'He will, in any case,' added Telford in an undertone, which Desmond, however, caught, and answered with a swift cuffing.

'Be at the Theatrical Soc meeting at

seven-thirty to-morrow, then,' McLaren said,
as he departed. 'And, I say, don't let
Wright's get to know about it, or they 'll
steal our stage costumes or something, like
they did last time. It 's working under diffi-
culties to get up a stunt with those chaps
hanging round, waiting for the first opportunity to rag us. So long!'

'You *are* touched, Des,' D'Arcy said, 'You
know you can't act.'

'Oh, leave him alone, Darkie,' the Tiger
said.

'But he knows *I* 'd make a better Macbeth,'
persisted D'Arcy.

'But not much better,' said Telford.

'No better! Here, I 'm going to get a
copy of the play and start swotting it up at
once!' Desmond announced, making for the
study window, his usual entrance.

'Well, there 's one thing,' D'Arcy said, as
Desmond ran across the tennis-courts, 'it 'll
take old Des's mind off Rix a bit. If ever
anyone was obsessed with anything, he 's
obsessed with Rix's woes. I can't understand it. Who is Rix, to be so attractive
to a chap like Des?'

'If you ask me, he 's a nasty bad-tempered
little owl,' replied Telford. 'But don't ask
me, because I never on any account say

anything disparaging of a chap behind his back.'

'Well, I'd like to hear you say that to Rix's face, that's all,' D'Arcy answered. 'If Rix had been as snubby to me as he's been to Desmond, I'd watch championing him. And as a rule, Des is very touchy too,' he went on. 'It's all beyond me.'

'You're rather thick,' answered Telford. 'There's the supper-bell.'

There wasn't much rehearsing done next evening, because the actors showed an inclination to fight over the parts. There were at least six fellows who asserted they could play Macbeth better than Henry Irving, but Desmond stuck to the part through thick and thin, even offering to uphold his rights with his two good fists. This last argument being too forcible, he was allowed to keep the part, and the next squabble was over Lady Macbeth. But Lestrange, being the best actor in St Martin's and also the most girlish in appearance, managed to keep that too, and in the end the rôles were still as McLaren had fixed them. Then they got to work, and after sundry drawbacks, such as being locked in the pavilion, where they were rehearsing, by one of Wright's chaps, and having all their copies of the play carried off and dropped into the junior baths, they had the play in acting order. Dr Newton was very pleased with their efforts. He gave them carte-blanche as to stage arrangements, and promised to excuse preparation on the night on which the play was acted. He also gave them many hints as to costumes, &c., and lent them a dagger and two swords, and provided a bottle of red ink for the necessary gore. Altogether, it seemed as though the thing was going to be a success.

There was but one fly in the ointment.

'What about Wright's?' asked Desmond, when they were fixing the chairs in the big hall for the audience. It was the afternoon before the evening arranged for the perform-ance. 'We've fixed their place at the back, but, all the same, they may boo or hiss or something.'

'They won't, old bean,' said D'Arcy. 'Look here!' He pointed to a large arm-chair which he had placed beside the seats reserved for Wright's House. On it was a notice, which said clearly: 'Reserved for Dr Newton.'

'But the Newt says he can't come till half-past eight,' said Desmond, 'and the show'll be half over by then.'

'Yes; but they don't know that, do they?

He may not sit here if he does come, but I bet that chair 'll do the trick. They 'll be expecting him every minute, and won't dare to try any stunts.'

'I don't know so much about that,' Desmond answered. 'But it 's worth trying, anyway. If they do hiss or anything, the School 'll be awfully down on them—it 'd be very unsporting. What I 'm afraid of is that they 'll get some more subtle means of messing the show up. They 've been suspiciously calm lately, and Robson gave me a particularly sweet smile this morning when we were going out of chapel.'

'Oh, don't think about it,' advised D'Arcy, 'or you 'll make a mess of it yourself through the very expectation.'

'I won't,' Desmond said. 'I 'll show them! You wait.'

'Well, I 'm glad you 're so self-confident,' D'Arcy laughed. 'Go on thinking Duncan is Robson, then you 'll make the murder most realistic.'

But the play opened most effectively. The three witches, chief of whom was Sefton, were three Fifth-form boys who did not know the meaning of the word 'nervousness.' Duncan was splendid, though his beard gave him a little trouble, certainly. But when

Desmond entered, clad in a skin jacket and rough short plaid and wearing a black wig, there was a great burst of cheering, the part of the hall occupied by Wright's making by principle a little oasis in it, until Allerick, O'Shane, and Hare started to clap louder than anyone else. Desmond seemed even taller than usual, his nervousness, which, in spite of his boast, was considerable, gave him just the rigid upright bearing which was necessary. He did not stammer—the applause gave him confidence—and his speech was perfectly clear, if rather expressionless. He was inclined to put the emphasis in the wrong places.

After the first scene things were delayed a little, because two members of Wright's Fifth-form waylaid young Long, the second witch, as he came from the dressing-room, and tried to prevent him reaching the stage. Long fought like a lion, and finally left his kidnappers sitting on the stairs moaning. He dashed on to the stage and the curtain went up.

'Where hast thou been, sister?' asked Sefton.

'Killing swine!' answered Long, with such gusto that a roar of laughter went up.

After that everything went as well as possible. Lestrange made such a wonderful Lady Macbeth that even Wright's clapped after the banquet scene. Desmond began to

act really well, and Allerick, who was sitting
just behind Dr Newton, heard the Head-
master remark to Mr Wright that he never
knew the boy had it in him. Allerick was
pleased that the Head-master had come in
late, and so had seen the best part of Desmond's performance.

So Act IV. commenced, with the witches'
recital of the horrors of the cauldron. The
fire beneath the cauldron was formed by an
electric torch placed under thin tissue-paper
and twigs. The cauldron was borrowed from
the School museum, and was a deep iron
affair which the three witches stirred with a
long wooden spoon.

Desmond came on the semi-dark stage,
cloaked heavily. 'How now, you secret,
black, and midnight hags, what is 't you
do?'

'A deed without a name,' chorused the
three, and Sefton gave the cauldron a particularly brisk stir. Immediately he did so
there was a faint pop, and there rose out of
the iron pot fumes which might certainly
have been formed by the fillet of a fenny
snake and all the other pleasant ingredients.
It was about the limit in smells, and set the
three witches coughing furiously. Most of
the audience thought the coughs were part

of the performance, but Desmond was taken aback. He approached the fire, making a desperate effort to gain his self-confidence, and the smell caught him, and therefore his speech went. 'I conjure you, by that which you profess (Howe'er you come to know it), answer me: Though you untie the winds and . . . My goodness—sulphuretted hydrogen!'

He could not go on. He was choked. The witches fled incontinently from the platform, and the stage-hand with great presence of mind tried to haul down the curtain, but in the haste it got stuck, and before it fell the fumes had reached the audience and were causing them to hold their noses.

Desmond, absolutely red with fury, clapped his cloak over his nostrils, and carrying the awful cauldron into the dressing-room ran the tap over it to dissolve the fumes. A toy balloon had been carefully filled with sulphuretted hydrogen gas and placed at the bottom of the cauldron, so that the first hard stir had burst it.

'Of all the filthy tricks!' Desmond said to D'Arcy, as he returned. 'But we're not going to let it stop the play, as it was evidently intended to do. Come on back. We're going on without the cauldron.'

But it was easier said than done. The tension

of the play was ruined, there was an uproar of talk and laughter in the hall, and by the time they had calmed it, the actors were in a fury of impatience.

The Head-master mounted the platform and, bravely ignoring the sulphuretted hydrogen which lingered in the atmosphere, gave his candid opinion of the mean trick, and said the play should continue. There was complete silence then, in which a little drama was acted at the back of the hall.

Allerick was sitting directly in front of Robson. As the Head-master left the platform and Desmond and the others reappeared, Robson gave a little cruel laugh at the captain of Leigh's red perspiring face. Allerick said nothing, but he turned round and struck Robson across the face. Robson's face went as white as a sheet and across it blazed the red imprint of Allerick's fingers. There was a sudden dumbfounded silence around the two.

'What do you mean by that?' asked Robson between set teeth.

'That's just to wipe the laugh off,' Allerick explained. 'But I'm quite willing to explain further, with or without gloves.'

'You sneaking cad!' Robson answered. 'Do you think I'd fight a——'

Dr Newton walked up to the row and took his seat. Robson's speech died and he tried to look calm. He put his hand up to his face to hide the finger-marks, but all the time his white even teeth were digging into his under-lip and his grey eyes were fixed on the stubby short hair at the back of Allerick's head. The actors never regained their enthusiasm, and it was just a case of getting the play over as quickly as possible. Desmond hardly said another line without stuttering, and when it was over he sat down on a locker in the dressing-room, ran his fingers through his hair, and rubbed his chin, two signs of his de-spondency. He tossed away his wig, but continued to wear the jacket and kilt, and it was dressed thus the Head-master found him.

'Well, Desmond, I've come to congratulate you,' the latter said. 'I didn't know you were an actor.'

Desmond's lip twisted bitterly, but he did not reply. He knew the Head wasn't sar-castic, but he wished he'd been left alone.

'That mean trick ruined the play, of course,' said Dr Newton; 'but everyone realised that. You ought to feel proud of yourself!' he smiled, as he went.

But Desmond didn't. 'I never felt more murderous in my life,' he said to D'Arcy.

'What on earth gave anyone the fiendish ingenuity for such a trick?'

'I'll answer you with apparent irrelevance,' said D'Arcy, 'with another bit of information. I've just met Pat O'Shane waddling around in a worried condition. If it wasn't too late, there'd be a fight on now. As it is, it's coming off first thing in the morning. Rix and Robson.'

'Rix and Robson? Why?'

'Robson laughed, and Allerick smacked his beautiful mug. They're both mad. It's going to be a fight worth seeing.'

Desmond's eyes became dark almost to blackness. He started to pull off the skin jacket. 'I give it up!' he said, and his tone was that of a man denouncing the whole world.

CHAPTER XIII.

ALLERICK IS KNOCKED OUT.

DESMOND awoke next morning with the depressing sensation that an unpleasant experience was before him. Then full recollection rushed upon him and he groaned to himself. Allerick was going to fight Robson before prayer-bell sounded. Well, he'd have to hurry. He was just fastening his tie when D'Arcy thrust his black head round the cubicle door.

'Hurry up, Des, if you're coming,' he said. 'I've just had a squint through the window, and saw Allerick making for the gym.'

'Oh, I wish I could stop this affair,' breathed Desmond. 'It's an awful thing—especially for Wright's.'

D'Arcy gave a soft meditative chuckle. 'You do play up your unselfish hero pose to perfection, Des,' he said. 'Ranger would have been in stitches at the thought of Wright's captain and Wright's ex-captain fighting like a couple of street urchins.'

'I wish Rix would call off.'

'He can't. He did the smacking. And I don't think Robson will. Rix stands to beat him, especially if it's with gloves.'

'I'll jolly well see it is!' Desmond snapped. 'There's going to be no fighting without. Come along.'

They dashed along the dormitory, and met Telford as he came out of his cubicle.

'Where are you off to?' asked Telford.

'Come with us and you'll see,' answered Desmond. And added to D'Arcy, 'He'll make one more to support Rix. Robson is bound to have half a dozen pals with him.'

All Wright's Sixth were in the gymnasium, excited and noisy.

Allerick stood between O'Shane and Hare, obviously waiting for something. When Desmond entered he strode forward. 'I'm glad you've come,' he said, and at his expression Desmond realised how wonderfully Allerick's feelings about him had changed in the last few weeks. 'I'm going to fight Robson.'

Robson strolled up to Desmond as though he had nothing to do, and all day to do it in. ''Morning, Desmond!' he said, with his most mocking smile. 'I suppose you made a special effort to be present? Trust Leigh's to be in anything that's essentially Wright's business.'

'I wouldn't be so clever, if I were you,' answered Desmond coldly. 'You won't feel like taking me on when Rix has finished with you.'

'When *I* have finished with Rix, I shall be happy to oblige!' retorted Robson, a gleam lighting his grey eyes for a second.

'Sounds as if you're going to make a good day's work,' Desmond laughed. 'Don't worry. You're safe as far as I'm concerned.'

'You funk it!' breathed Robson.

For answer, Desmond turned his back on Robson and walked across to Allerick. 'Are you determined to go on with this, Rix?' he asked. 'Why bother to fight the chap? He's not worth it.'

Allerick picked up a pair of boxing-gloves from the corner and commenced to try them on. In his shirt sleeves he looked much thinner and slighter than Robson, and when he removed his spectacles Desmond saw the dark rings of worry beneath his fine eyes. 'I've got to go on with it, Des,' he said. 'There's no other way of relieving the matter. I couldn't help hitting, and I can't help going on with it now. If you think I'm doing something wrong, don't stay and countenance it,' he added, with weary spite. 'I wouldn't offend your dignity or your conscience for the world.'

Desmond's face crimsoned. He had actually turned to go when Allerick's hand shot out and grasped his arm:

'I'm sorry,' Allerick said. 'Don't know what makes me say such things. Be a good chap and stay.'

'Of course I will,' answered Desmond. 'I'm sorry you're going to fight; but as long as you are, I'm with you,' he added rather clumsily. But Allerick knew what he meant.

'O'Shane's my second,' said Allerick, and climbed into the ring. Robson followed, still smiling, and then Gregory, who was to referee.

Desmond thought at first that Robson was bound to win, Allerick was so much slighter, and a much poorer boxer. But Allerick fought with a wild persistence that was lacking in Robson, whose blows, when they got home, were almost casual. It seemed rather as if Robson were prolonging the fight by keeping merely on the defensive. He dodged Allerick's lunges, and tapped back, that was all. But he kept fresh, whereas Allerick's breath shortened to gasps, and beads of perspiration stood out on his forehead. So things continued for three rounds, after each of which

O'Shane mopped Allerick's face and told him
to go slower and be more careful. But
Allerick seemed deaf to all advice. He
turned to look round at Desmond as he rose
for the fourth round, and in his glance
Desmond saw the old wild fury, and was
glad that this time it was not for him.

But Robson changed his tactics and, as
though he were taking an interest in the fight
for the first time, he put in some hard blows
that made Allerick reel. Allerick managed a
quick left on Robson's chin that gave him an
opening, and he drove Robson back with a
rain of fierce blows. Robson sank against the
ropes, his fair hair tangled into damp locks,
his grey eyes half-closed, and Allerick stood
on guard waiting. But only Desmond saw
exactly what happened next. Everyone else
saw the fists, Desmond saw the feet. Robson
ran into the centre of the ring, Allerick met
him with a right-handed blow on the chest, and
as the two closed in together, Robson's foot
shot out, then his fist. He apparently knocked
Allerick out with a left-handed blow on the
chin, in reality he tripped him up. Allerick
fell against the corner of the ring and his head
caught the upright bar. He rolled over and
lay perfectly still, and so the fight ended.

But Desmond did not wait for the count.

He was up in the ring confronting Robson. 'You fouled!' he shouted. 'You cad, you tripped him up!'

Robson raised his eyebrows and looked round at the others as if to ask whether Desmond was mad.

'What on earth are you gibbering about?' asked Gregory. 'Rob couldn't help Allerick's head banging the post. Upon my word, is there *no* sportsmanship in Leigh's?'

'Be quiet!' broke in O'Shane suddenly, looking up with a face almost as white as Allerick's. 'I—can't—bring—him—round...'

Desmond ignored Gregory's taunt and dropped down on his knees beside Allerick. Allerick's face was ashen, and his lips blue. O'Shane was sponging his friend's forehead, and Desmond saw the Irishman's fingers tremble. 'He's all right, Pat,' he said. 'Lift his head up.'

O'Shane obeyed, and where Allerick's head had struck the post, Desmond found a slight cut, and held the sponge to it. 'We'd better take him to his cube,' he said; 'and if he's not better by prayers, we must send for Gray.'

He looked up and met Robson's eyes. Unaccountably he remembered the morning when Robson had stood thus and looked down at little Black. His fists clenched. 'Come on, Pat,' he said, lifting Allerick up, and together they carried him out of the gymnasium.

The members of Wright's did not seem very hilarious about Robson's triumph. There was something in the limp state of Allerick's body that damped their joy.

'He's all right,' said Robson. 'Trust Leigh's to make a martyr of him. Desmond had the cheek to say I fouled!' He laughed derisively.

'Don't take any notice of Desmond,' Gregory said. 'He's got Allerick on the brain.'

Robson slowly fastened his jacket, and as he did so the prayer-bell rang. 'Those fools'll be late for chapel if they start messing about after Allerick,' he said. 'Serve them right too. Come along, Greg. I'm sorry Allerick banged into that post; it spoilt the fight. I suppose O'Shane and the rest'll always say he'd have beaten me if he hadn't done that. But he wouldn't have done it.'

'Oh, you had him on toast,' answered Gregory, as they strolled away.

Desmond came into chapel late, with Hare and D'Arcy, but O'Shane and Allerick did not come at all. The captain of Leigh's looked very worried as he took his place, and he was the first to leave the chapel afterwards. He dashed straight into Wright's and up to the dormitory. O'Shane met him at the door. 'I'm going for Gray,' he said. 'Rix hasn't budged yet.'

Desmond strode into Allerick's cubicle. Allerick lay as one dead. 'He's stunned,' he said. 'Better get Gray, then. I'll stay here while you go.'

'But what can we say?' O'Shane inquired anxiously.

'Say he fell and knocked his head,' answered Desmond. 'It's the truth, even if it's not the whole truth. We can't let it out that he was fighting. Anyway, Robson fouled.'

'Are you sure of that, Des?'

'As sure as you stand here, Robson tripped Rix up. I'm certain now of Robson's character, whereas before . . . But clear off, Pat, there's no use standing talking.'

O'Shane hurried away, and Desmond stood beside the bed gazing down at Allerick's unconscious form. It seemed about an hour, in reality it was only five minutes later that O'Shane reappeared, accompanied by Dr Gray. The two boys watched anxiously while the doctor examined Allerick's head, lifted an eyelid, and sounded his pulse.

'He's cut his head badly in a nasty spot. These boys are always doing something.— He fell, you said, O'Shane? Larking, I suppose?'

'No, he wasn't larking,' said Desmond, wishing he could control the rich colour that flooded his cheeks so readily.

'It must have been a very heavy fall, anyway. And the boy was run down, too. Worried and played out. Over-studying, I suppose.' He bandaged Allerick's head, then ordered Desmond and O'Shane to go and tell the Head-master. 'Tell Dr Newton I'm seeing to him, but he won't be fit for school to-day, at any rate.'

'Won't he—is he still unconscious, sir?'

'Of course he is. And will be for some time, and when he becomes conscious probably he will wish he's unconscious again. One isn't able to take a lump out of one's scalp for fun, you know, Desmond.'

'No, sir,' answered Desmond. 'Thank you, sir.'

He went, and O'Shane and he made straight for the Head's study, meeting Dr Newton in the passage. 'Good-morning, boys!' he said, smiling cheerfully. 'Well?'

'We—er—we . . .' began Desmond, and then gave a glance of appeal at O'Shane.

'Dr Gray asked us to tell you about Allerick, sir. He's hurt his head and won't be able to take lessons to-day,' said O'Shane calmly.

'Hurt his head? How did he do that?' inquired the Head-master in concern. His glance fell on Desmond, whose colour again deepened to a rich crimson. O'Shane was at a loss for a moment, then he answered, 'He fell and struck the back of his head against something, sir, and cut it rather badly. Dr Gray is seeing to him, but he is still unconscious.'

'This is very serious,' said the Head-master. 'I must go up and see him. Thank you, boys.' He hurried away towards the stairs.

'I'd better go and see Whiskers before lessons,' said O'Shane. 'He'll be wondering how Rix is. So long, Des.'

'So long,' answered Desmond abstractedly, and stood still when O'Shane had gone, staring with unseeing eyes across the hall. Then suddenly, as if awakening out of a dream, he drew himself up and strode down the passage to his study. D'Arcy was seated at the table with about seven books round him, at none of which he was looking.

'Hullo!' Desmond cried. 'I thought it was French for your first lesson.'

'Old Guillaume's gone off groggy, so we were told to write a sonnet in the style of De Vigny. I 've never read any De Vigny, so I 'm going to write it in the style of the " Gaunt Stranger" instead. How 's old Rix ?'

' Still dead to the world,' answered Desmond with apparent callousness. Then he found an apple in the cupboard and devoured it savagely. 'Well, I 've no first lesson; let 's go on to the field. We can practise bowling.'

' No, we can't—or Leigh 'll see us through the window and want to know if that 's a new way of doing French. Come on to the tennis-courts, though, if you like.'

' Righto. I 've something to tell you, Darkie.' Desmond threw the core of the apple into the grate with a savage movement, and turned to his friend with a repellent glower.

' Great Scott !' D'Arcy laughed. ' Whatever 's up ?'

They jumped through the window and crossed the courts to a rustic-seat that stood against the shrubbery. Behind the shrubbery was the path to the swimming-baths.

Desmond looked round; there was no one in sight. ' Look here, D'Arcy,' he said. ' I 'm fed up with this business of Allerick.'

' How many more times are you going to say that ?' retorted D'Arcy. ' You 've said it half a dozen times an hour for the last three weeks. But you never seem to get any further.'

'Well, I'm going to get a bit further now. This foul play on Robson's part is about the last straw. He fouled. I saw him. And look here, Darkie,' Desmond's voice dropped, 'he hates Allerick. He searched Allerick's study. He found the medallion. Do you know what I think?'

'Something exciting, I dare say; but I happen to know all this.'

Desmond waved D'Arcy's protest aside impatiently. 'I don't think Robson *did* find the medallion in Rix's desk!' he breathed.

'No; it was Spencer, wasn't it?'

'Oh, you *thick* ass! Don't you see? Are you blind? Robson went to look at the collection just in front of Rix. He said the medallion was there. He *said* it.'

'Are you saying,' D'Arcy broke in, 'that Robson stole the medallion?'

''S-sh—be quiet.' Desmond glanced round. 'If ever this suspicion gets round, we stand absolutely no chance of putting things straight. We know Rix didn't steal the medallion, don't we?'

'Well, you seem pretty certain about it, old man,' D'Arcy murmured aggravatingly.

'Oh, do be serious, Darkie. Rix *isn't* a thief. Well, that leaves Robson or me. I'm not.'

'Aren't you?' smiled D'Arcy. 'I say, Des, don't get so worried. The thing's been going on for months. Surely, it can go on a bit longer.'

'It can't. I can't see Robson in Rix's place. Robson is a cad and a sneak. Why shouldn't he be a——'

'But this cuts no ice. What can you do?'

'I've got an idea. I've been thinking too much of what can't be done. I can't tell the Newt my suspicions. I can't confront Robson. But I can go to Dowling and get a bit more truth out of him.'

'Oh, I say! Draw it mild. The Newt questioned him.'

'I have a feeling there was a lot the Newt didn't get out of old man Dowling. Without meaning to bring your little pet author into it, I must say Dowling is a sinister man.'

'But the Newt'd be so ratty if——'

'Let the Newt be ratty,' Desmond said. 'It's only the thought of what the Newt'd think that's kept me from doing this before. I'm going to-night. I'm not thinking of myself any more——'

'Sorry I haven't a V.C. in my pocket with

which to decorate you,' D'Arcy answered.
'It's evidently what you're expecting.   Well,
fire ahead.   Only don't forget what the Newt
said about the results being drastic for anyone
who wasn't in at call-over.   It's because of
this fair at Calleridge.'

'Well, I'm not going anywhere near
Calleridge, am I?   And I'll be back by call-
over easily.   I'll go right after prep.'

'I'll come too,' D'Arcy offered eagerly.

'No, thank you.   This is my show.   You're
too excitable.'

'Thank you,' said D'Arcy, quite undismayed
by Desmond's blunt refusal.   'You do cheer
a fellow up.   Well, your blood be on your
own head.   My great brains might have been
of service.   And I know Dowling better than
you do.   I used to buy post-cards from him.'

'You must know him well, then,' smiled
Desmond sarcastically.   'No; I'm sorry,
Darkie, but this isn't a lark.'

'Nothing's ever a lark to you now.   You're
as serious as an undertaker since you were
made captain of Leigh's.   I've not had one
good laugh out of you this term.'

'There hasn't been much to laugh at,
certainly; but——'

'That used never to make any difference.
Oh, there's the bell.'   He jumped up, caught

his foot in a tuft of grass, and fell backwards
into a gorse-bush, so comically that Desmond
let out a great roar of laughter.   D'Arcy
staggered up, painfully pricked.   'I thought
you'd lost your sense of humour!' he snapped,
glaring at Desmond; then he laughed too, and
they raced each other to the study window.

When they had gone there was a slight
movement from the bushes behind, and the
quick patter of plimsoled feet on the gravel
path.

Robson wore a worried frown, then he
smiled his peculiar slow cruel smile and went
into the School.   Strange he should just
manage to overhear that interesting conversation.

But more than one person can eavesdrop,
as Robson was soon to learn to his cost.

CHAPTER XIV.

MR DOWLING ENTERTAINS A VISITOR.

DESMOND'S face wore a look of great determination as he swung down the village street that evening. More than one person turned to take another glance at him, for he was no ordinary figure, being so tall and erect. His cap was pushed rakishly to one side, and his hands were thrust deep into his blazer-pockets, and his fearless eyes burned their deepest blue as he concentrated on the interview before him.

When he reached Dowling's shop he stood and gazed into the window until he was quite sure there was no business going on inside, then he strode in, pursing his lips and trying to look very important.

Mr Dowling was bending over a case of quaint old rings. He was very bent and grey, and Desmond wondered what chance he would have if a big ruffian—say, his own size—chose to call on him in the quiet of the evening. But when Mr Dowling looked up and saw the college cap, a queer glint came into the eyes

behind the spectacles that made Desmond
think that they were not quite so short-
sighted as their owner gave one to believe.
There is something very harmless and respectable in short-sight due to old age.

‘ Well, sir ? ’ asked Mr Dowling in his high
cracked voice. ‘ It ’s a fine evening, isn’t it ? ’
He shot the question at Desmond with curious
eagerness, as if the weather were the most
important topic in the world.

Desmond had an impulse to buy a picture
post-card and clear out as quickly as he could,
but he stifled it and cleared his throat.
‘ Very fine,’ he answered. ‘ W-would it be
possible for me to have a word with you in
private ? ’

Mr Dowling came round the counter till he
was close to Desmond, facing him. The
countless tiny wrinkles round his eyes fas-
cinated the boy, who wondered what age
could add them all. Mr Dowling’s coat was
very old and dusty, and the hands he spread
before him on the counter were grimy in spite
of their many rings. ‘ And what may be your
name, young sir ? ’ he asked. He studied
Desmond from foot to head, appraising him
as one does a work of art.

‘ Neville Desmond.’

‘ I don’t know the name ; but you ’re a fine

young fellow. You'll not mind me saying so?'

Desmond's chin went up just a little, but Dowling noticed. 'Perhaps you want to tell me something very important—too important to be said in the shop, eh?' he inquired, and gave a queer little ripple of laughter that somehow confirmed Desmond's opinion that he was sinister. 'Well, I don't often get visits from young college gentlemen—though there's one as buys moths, and occasionally they come to sell things.' He looked intently at Desmond. 'Ah well,' he added in a low voice, 'we all get hard up sometimes and glad to sell something—anything, however precious it may be. Most of these things around you, sir, were the last thing their owners wished to part with.'

'You haven't told me whether I can speak to you in private,' Desmond said with some impatience. 'I have not much time to spare.' He glanced at his watch with an unconscious touch of hauteur.

'Come into my parlour,' said Dowling. 'I'll call Percival to mind the shop.' He went round a screen and called Percival, whereat a boy of sixteen, very pale, thin, and foppish-looking, appeared. 'I'm just going in with this gentleman—Mr Desmond,' said Dowling.

Percival looked at Desmond and then at

the shopkeeper. 'Right, I'll mind the shop,' said he, and sat down at the counter.

Desmond disliked Percival at sight, and he disliked even more the dark passage that was revealed when Mr Dowling opened the door. It smelt musty, and was crowded with suits of armour and stuffed heads of animals. 'Like the Old Curiosity Shop!' thought Desmond, and reflected that Mr Dowling was not at all like Nell's grandfather.

'Growing dusk!' croaked Mr Dowling behind him, as if the outside light could possibly make any difference to the windowless passage. 'Straight on. That's right. There's the door. Only a small place, young sir, but you'll find it very cosy.'

A curious emphasis on the last words gave Desmond a throb of misgiving, and the moment he had stepped inside the room he swung round. But he was too late. The door slammed in his face, there was the quick grating of a key, and Dowling's low chuckle from the passage. 'Very, very cosy!' he went on. 'And you'll be there till well after call-over, which is something pleasant to think about.'

'What on earth are you doing?' cried Desmond, rattling the lock savagely. 'Why have you locked me in?'

'Spies must expect to be locked up, my young Lord Airs and Graces,' was the answer. ' A little bird told me that you came to ask an awkward question.'

'There'll be awkward questions asked when I tell Dr Newton why I wasn't in at call-over!' retorted Desmond, his voice hoarse with fury. 'Very awkward.'

'Very awkward,' agreed Dowling. 'Aha, I sympathise with you. Yes, the Headmaster will want to know what you were doing here.'

'I came to get the truth about the person who tried to sell you the Necra medallion,' Desmond said. 'And if you knew what I came for you are making the case black against yourself by treating me like this. My friend knows I came here and will lose no time in coming for me.'

'Oh, I won't keep you here for ever!' answered the croaking voice, with a little chuckle. 'Just long enough to cool you down a little and bring you to reason.'

'What's your game? Do you want to get money out of me?'

'Oh no; I have plenty of money. I have so much money I could have bought the Necra medallion if I had wished. I could have given quite a lot of money to—Mr Allerick.'

Desmond sank heavily against the door, with the sensation of an icy hand clutching his throat. 'You liar!' he stammered, trembling so that his voice shook. 'Who told you that name?'

'Better ask no questions,' was the answer. 'Sometimes inquisitive persons get more than they bargain for. Perhaps it would have been better if you had not been so eager to emulate the great Sherlock Holmes. You see——'

'It was *not* Allerick,' said Desmond. 'And I'll get the truth out of you before I'm much older.'

'You have all the truth now—the Headmaster had the description of the thief, and you have the name. Why not fit them together? The result would be so pleasant for my dear friend Mr Allerick!' He hobbled down the passage, still chuckling, as though he had made the best joke in the world.

Desmond found a stool beside him and sank on to it, clutching his brown hair in an agony of bewilderment. Allerick? Allerick? What did it mean? Allerick was the thief after all. A thief and a liar, and a hypocrite into the bargain; a fellow who could smile and lie and shake hands while his mind was plotting further deception. Then suddenly it seemed as if a vision of Allerick's ugly face and sincere

steady eyes rose before Desmond's mind.
' No, it 's not Allerick ! ' he said almost aloud.
' If half England came on their knees and
swore it was Rix I 'd not believe them.
There 's a catch somewhere. I must think.
No ; what 's the use of sitting thinking ? I
must get out and be back by call-over, or the
Head 'll find out. He 'll be angry because
I 've presumed to further his inquiries. But
suppose Dowling mentions Allerick's name ?
And why is the old madman keeping me here ? '

He studied the room as well as he could
in the dim light, and soon decided that
there was no chance of escape through the
window—it was too high and too narrow ;
moreover, barred. He was not in a parlour,
but some sort of storeroom, filled with dirty
packing-cases and cardboard boxes containing
musty papers. Opposite him, beneath the
window, was a long mirror, giving an uncanny
reflection of his white face and striped blazer.

He crept to the door and listened, but there
was no sound at all. Passing his fingers over
the lock he discovered four large screws, one
at each corner. Suppose he unscrewed them
would the door open ? Provided there was
no additional lock or bolt they would. It
was worth trying, anyway. His penknife
was in his blazer-pocket, but at the first twist

in the screw he broke the point of the blade.
Afterwards, however, he was able to fit it into
the screw.   It was hard work, but he managed
to get out the four screws.   After poking at
the surrounding woodwork for some time he
lifted out the lock.   'Well, that was easy!'
smiled Desmond, as he cautiously opened
the door.   But how to pass through the
shop?

He had decided to creep to the far door,
and once there, make a dash for the road,
when he heard the murmur of a conversation
coming from the shop.   Something in the
voice speaking struck familiarly on his ear.
He could not distinguish any words.   Nearer
he crept to the other door, nearer still, walking
carefully for fear he tripped over any of the
litter on the floor.   What a good thing he
had rubber soles on his heavy golf-shoes!
Then he reached the door—it was slightly
ajar.   He got close to one of the suits of
armour and leant against the wall, scarcely
daring to breathe.

Old Dowling was speaking now.   'I'll have
to shut up the shop in a few minutes, but
I'll let him out the back way.'

'Where is he?'

It was Robson's voice!   Desmond's heart
gave a great thump, and he had to clench

his fists to keep from shouting. He exerted
all his powers of control, and forgetting he
was eavesdropping, strained his ears to catch
every word of what was being said.

'He's in the storeroom,' was the answer.
'And not very pleased with life, either. Fine
young figure of a chap.' Mr Dowling's
voice was neither cracked nor hoarse now,
yet Desmond recognised it.

'You gave him to understand that it was
Allerick who offered you the medallion?'
Robson's voice was cold and masterful.

'Yes; and he called me a liar.'

'A sign that he believed you. He cares
for Allerick, you know. Allerick's being
chucked out will be a great blow to him,
that's why I want it to happen. I've hated
Allerick always, but now I think I hate
Desmond more. Well, he'll be late for call-
over, and he won't tell the Head where
he's been. I know him. He'll stick to
Allerick's innocence till he's deceiving himself. But I'll make him pay up more than
that!' Robson laughed as though the pros-
pect pleased him immensely.

A cold shiver ran down Desmond's back,
and suddenly he could restrain himself no
longer. He swung open the door and came
face to face with Robson.

Robson went white to the lips, but he did not flinch. 'Look out!' he called suddenly, as Desmond moved forward.

With astonishing rapidity Mr Dowling reached the front door and closed it.

'We can't let you go, you see, Desmond,' smiled Robson; 'especially as you seem to have been taking an interest in my little peroration. I'm sorry it upheld so nobly the tradition that listeners never hear any good of themselves.'

'I should think it *was* good that you should hate me,' answered Desmond, outwardly as calm as Robson himself. 'I should think you would hate me, you low sneaking cad! Don't think you're not caught now. I've seen your game right through, and Dr Newton will see it too.'

'When?' asked Robson. Then he turned to look at Dowling as he stood by the door, and there was a menacing gleam in his eyes.

Desmond strode to the door. 'You'd better let me pass,' he said to Dowling. 'Your game's up.'

'Oh, not quite,' smiled Mr Dowling; 'because you can't tell the Head without going back to the School, can you? And you're certainly not going to do that.'

'I don't want to knock an old man down,' Desmond answered, 'but I shall do so if you do not let me pass.' There was a wild light in his blue eyes now. He had seen the youth Percival come from behind the screen and take his place in the centre of the shop. Three to one.

Robson made a quick movement forward to reach the door. Desmond thrust Dowling down with one sweep of his huge arm, and would have been out of the door in a second had not the old man seized hold of his legs. Before he could shake off the clutch, Robson and Percival were upon him. Percival's hands went round his neck to pull him backwards, and Robson gave his arms a fiendish twist that made him scream with pain.

'Oh, you'll have quite a lot to tell Dr Newton when next you see him!' Robson said. 'But it won't be for a long while yet.'

Desmond gasped for breath and tried to struggle upwards, but he was helpless. Robson sat on his chest while the other two tied his arms and legs.

'This is great fun, isn't it?' inquired Robson, smiling down into his enemy's blazing eyes. 'Isn't it D'Arcy who is so fond of reading

the works of Mr Edgar Wallace? Well, by
the time we 've finished with you, you'll be
able to write a book on the same lines for
him.'

'Don't—be—mad,' panted Desmond. 'I
tell you Darkie knows I 've come here. As
soon as call-over is over and he misses me
he 'll go to the Newt.'

'Will he?' Robson answered. 'And I
wonder what the Newt will think of you being
here? Or, I should say,' he added, 'of you
not being here—for you won't be here by
the time the search-party arrives.'

'Are you trying to scare me?' Desmond
broke out; 'because it doesn't work.'

'Oh we 're not going to stab you and
sink you in the river, my dear chap!' laughed
Robson. 'Don't get that into your head.
Not quite so Wallacian as all that. But
you 're just going to stay with dear Mr
Dowling for a few hours, or even a few
days, until I receive the proceeds from the
sale of the Necra medallion, which is being
conducted by one of his agents in London.'

'Are you mad?' asked Desmond. 'The
Necra medallion has been returned to its
owner long ago. You placed it yourself in
Allerick's writing-case, where you pretended
to find it.'

'Oh, you *are* clever, Desmond!' laughed Robson, and Mr Dowling and Percival joined in the laugh, greatly amused. 'Who'd steal a fifty-thousand-pound medallion just for the joy of putting it in another fellow's writing-case?'

'You hate Allerick. You wanted him to go. You wanted to be captain of Wright's.'

'Not quite so much as I wanted the fifty-thousand that the Necra medallion would bring,' Robson answered. 'But you have certainly grasped my feelings towards Allerick accurately. I was very pleased to get him chucked out. I'd be more pleased to get you chucked out, only, unfortunately, I haven't time to stop and see it. I find the climate at St Martin's doesn't agree with me, so I am taking a—er—Mediterranean cruise. Very pleasant. You see, in his joy at recovering the Necra medallion, Lord Inverslowe will probably not examine it too closely; but when he does so, he will make the unpleasant discovery that it is not eleven hundred years old, but merely a fortnight. Perhaps you do not grasp my meaning, but if you think it over I am sure you will understand that there are rubies *and* rubies, Desmond; also a very useful substance known as glass. And now, as your broad manly chest is beginning

to make a rather uncomfortable settee, and
also as you are getting purple in the face
and breathing stertorously, which troubles
me, for I hate to give anyone pain, I will
arise and go—not to Innisfree, but to my little
white bed within St Martin's ancient walls.
And dear kind Mr Dowling and his nephew
will look after you and make you comfortable.' He rose, and looked down at Desmond's white face with the most mocking of
smiles.

Desmond's eyes were closed, for his brain
was spinning and he was on the verge of
unconsciousness.

'Good-night, Desmond,' Robson ended;
and the very depths of his nature being
revealed, he kicked the captain of Leigh's
as he lay there, and laughed when Desmond
groaned. 'I'll see you again soon, Dowling,'
he said, as he unbolted the door. 'I wouldn't
go back, only there's a craze in me that is
gratified by the thought of sitting on the
edge of a volcano's crater. And let me
know first post in the morning, about—you
know what. And for goodness' sake, keep
this fellow safe till then; and don't let him
get out again, or he'll make himself a more
serious nuisance.' He strode out into the
street. The dying sun caught his shining

hair and made a kind of halo round it as he walked away, careless and half smiling.

'He's a cool card, that 'un,' said young Percival appreciatively. 'Did you see how calm he was when this chap landed out so suddenly?   Must be good to have nerves like that one's.'

'Ay,' said Dowling, 'he's like his father; never turns a hair.   Looks as if Desmond's gone off it.   Shouldn't wonder.'

'He's taken the lock clean out of the storehouse door,' said Percival.   'We'll have to get it back before the people from the School come to make inquiries, or they may ask awkward questions.'

'That's so.   Here, help me to drag this chap into the cellar.   My, what a weight he is!'

As they laid their hands upon him, Desmond opened dazed eyes and made a last struggle to get free; but it was useless, the ropes which bound him were tied in good hard knots.   He gave up the attempt, and after saying, 'You'll be sorry for this,' he made no further effort to move or to speak.

They dragged him round the screen down three stairs into a small kitchen.   In the centre of this room was a large heavy rug. Percival rolled this on one side, revealing a

small trap-door, which he raised. A flight
of wooden stairs was disclosed, and down
these Desmond was bundled with little
gentleness. He was placed on the floor of
the cellar with his back to the wall.

'Aren't you going to untie the ropes?'
asked Percival.

''Twouldn't be safe,' answered his uncle.
'He's such a big chap, he'd knock us both
down easily.'

'How will he eat and drink?'

'Oh, he'll manage to eat right enough.
He's not tied so securely as that, and he'll
have plenty of time to learn how to do it.
Get a cob of bread and a jug of milk,
Percy? We can't let him starve, anyway.
Isn't he a young giant?'

'Pretty big,' answered Percival nonchalantly;
'it took three of us to hold him, anyhow.'
He found the simple food and drink, and
placed them on the floor beside Desmond.
'There's plenty of air, you won't suffocate,'
he said, pointing to a tiny opening in the
wall high up in the far corner.

Desmond needed the assurance, the air
was heavy and not too pleasant in flavour,
and the floor felt damp. He raised his
bound hands to brush the hair from his forehead. As Dowling and Percival remounted

the stairs he had a sudden fit of terror, and wanted to cry, 'Don't leave me alone here!'

But he remained silent, and Dowling looked round as he reached the top step, to see his prisoner sitting glaring into the dimness, his eyes as fearless as ever.

CHAPTER XV.

MISSING.

O'SHANE strolled across to Leigh's that evening about half-past eight and put his thin troubled face round the door of Study 7. D'Arcy, now the preparation period was over, had finished his murder mystery and was starting the unusual task of doing his French exercise, for the simple reason that he had no one to whom to talk. Therefore he was pleased to see O'Shane, and closed his book the minute he entered.

'Where's Des?' inquired O'Shane.

'Gone down the road,' answered D'Arcy vaguely, for Desmond's last words had been: 'On your life, don't tell anyone where I am, Darkie. If anything happens, I'll do my own explaining.'

'Can I come in?' asked the Irishman.

'You're in, son. What's the trouble? You look as if the Free State border had been abolished, or something.'

'It's old Rix—I got tired of messing round alone. Whiskers is at choir practice.

They can't get him out of the choir. He's impervious to hints, and his voice is like an old gramophone with a broken needle.' O'Shane murmured the words abstractedly, as though he were thinking of other things; and, sitting down, commenced to examine D'Arcy's tennis racquet, which lay casually on the floor.

'How's old Rix?' inquired D'Arcy; but because he was busy drawing a portrait of Charlie Chaplin on the back of De Vigny, he did not notice the queer spasm which crossed O'Shane's face.

'Haven't you heard?'

'Not a thing.'

'He's come round.'

'Good egg.'

'It isn't good egg,' O'Shane answered. 'He's frightfully ill—he——'

D'Arcy glanced quickly up, his black eyes losing their mischievous gleam. 'Here, tell a chap!' he exclaimed. 'What's up?'

'He's gone—er—wonky on top—can't remember things properly—says daft things . . .' O'Shane gave the screw of the racquet-press a violent twist and subsided into miserable silence.

D'Arcy's face paled. 'D' you mean he's not all there?'

'Dr Gray says he'll be all right in a day or two, but they've sent for his mater. He's got no pater, you know.'

'Has he lost his memory?'

'He can't remember the fight—at least— he's got such a queer idea—I mean—oh, perhaps he'll be all right to-morrow. He did get an awful bang, you know.'

D'Arcy made no answer; and, after a minute, O'Shane went on, trying to appear less concerned. 'He seems to think he was fighting Desmond.'

'What?' D'Arcy sat bolt-upright. 'Great Scott!'

'Frightful, isn't it?' O'Shane muttered. 'Oh, I could kill Robson cheerfully. You know Des said he fouled?'

'Yes; Des saw him. The cad! Well, perhaps he'll have a bit of remorse now. Who told you Allerick thought that, Pat?'

'Gray. He thought it was true. He rowed me for saying Rix fell, so I told him the truth. Not that Robson fouled, I don't mean, though I even felt like spouting that out too. Robson deserves it, in all conscience.'

There came a knock at the door, and Dr Gray himself entered. 'Will one of you ask Desmond to come up to the sanatorium immediately?' he asked.

'Desmond's out, sir,' answered D'Arcy.

'When will he be back?'

'Not till call-over, I think.'

'That's a nuisance. Well, send him up to the sanatorium as soon as he comes. Allerick has got some queer notion that he wants to "explain," and I can't get the young beggar to sleep. I don't want to give him a drug, and perhaps if he sees Desmond he'll be relieved of this obsession. Desmond's a sensible fellow, anyhow.'

The Doctor suddenly pounced on O'Shane, and lifted up his face to peer into it. 'You're worrying,' he said.

'Well, who wouldn't?' asked O'Shane quite indignantly.

'If there's one thing you're famous for, son,' went on the Doctor, 'it's for your habit of saying "Why worry?" Well, you're so clever telling other people, try a little of it on yourself. You sitting groaning won't help Allerick. You should have stopped him from making a fool of himself before. Anyway, Allerick'll probably be better when he's slept.—Now, D'Arcy, drag this doleful lump of Antrim round the field a few times, and tell him some jokes about Scots-

men. And don't forget to pack Desmond
off to me. Good-night.' Dr Gray took his
departure, leaving the other two considerably
cheered.

'Gray doesn't seem very cut up,' D'Arcy
said. 'Perhaps it's quite usual for chaps to
go wonky on top when they get a bang.
What d'you call it—concussion? You often
hear of it.'

'Yes.' O'Shane rose, stretching himself.
'Well, come on the field, then, Darkie.
Have you finished work?'

'Haven't started,' was the answer, 'but
that's a detail.'

They climbed through the window on to
the tennis-courts.

'Des'll be awfully cut up about Rix
thinking that,' D'Arcy said. 'You know,
Pat, he thinks Rix is little Lord Pot.'

'You have an elegant way of putting it,'
smiled O'Shane. 'Can't you see anything in
Rix to account for Des being so keen on
him?'

'What an awkward question to ask a
chap,' D'Arcy said. 'But since you press
me—no. I like Rix all right, you know,
but—I say, there's Robson. Looks as if
he's going to speak to us.'

'I hope he doesn't,' O'Shane breathed.

But Robson, slipping through the hedge to save going round to the gate, came straight up to them, smiling pleasantly. 'I thought I'd come and ask how poor Allerick's getting on,' he said quietly.

O'Shane's eyes wore an unusual expression of fury. 'He's jolly ill—thanks to you!'

Robson's smile faded. 'Oh, how rotten,' he said. 'But don't blame me, Pat——'

'My name is O'Shane.'

'O'Shane, then, if you prefer it. I didn't want Allerick to cut his head, you know. And it was Allerick who started the fight.'

'Yes, and he'd probably have finished it but for your foot,' retorted D'Arcy, unable to remain silent, though he wanted to appear contemptuous of Robson.

'What do you mean?' questioned Robson, but his fingers were beating a strange little tattoo against his knee.

'You fouled,' said O'Shane. 'And anything that happens to Allerick is at your door.' He thought perhaps Robson would be frightened, but if he was he did not show it.

'That's a beastly thing to say, O'Shane,' Robson said; 'and if I didn't know you are worried about Allerick, I'd make you pay up for it. It was a perfectly fair fight—Rix

was just too mad and hasty, that's all. But
if you're going to believe all Desmond
says . . .' He shrugged his shoulders, and
with a sort of half-smile walked away.

'He did well to make off then,' D'Arcy
said. 'I would have smacked his face too
if he'd called Des a liar. Do you notice, all
these quarrels seem to be over Des, and yet
Des himself is always preaching good-will,
and so on?'

'Part of the irony of life,' answered O'Shane.
'But I never *did* meet a term like this one—
theft, fouled matches, fouled fights—Jove!
I'm glad it's nearly over.'

'There's the Cranfield match next Saturday,' D'Arcy answered. 'Let's hope nothing
happens to spoil that.'

'I shouldn't wonder if it did, everything
seems to be going wrong.'

'Oh, don't be so cheerful! Let's get the
racquets and have a set. You can borrow
Desmond's. Come on.'

They were still playing tennis when the
bell for call-over went, and the exercise
raised their spirits.

D'Arcy stopped as he was about to serve.
'I say, what shall we do? Des hasn't come
back.'

'You answer his *adsum* for him.'

'I can't. The Newt always looks at him
as he calls his name. Looks as if Des is
going to cop it.'

'But where's he gone?' persisted O'Shane.

'He told me not to say.'

'The Newt'll want to know.'

'He'll have to want,' answered D'Arcy
elegantly. 'But there's old Rix worrying
himself to death. Come on, then; it's no
use our being late too. Perhaps Des'll turn
up at the last minute and go straight into
hall.' D'Arcy looked worried. He wished
Desmond had let him go to Dowling's too.
He was going to be in a fix if the Head-
master asked any questions. What was
Desmond doing that he was so long away?

But he was to be more worried ere the
evening was over. Dr Newton noticed Desmond's absence as soon as he entered the
hall. Dr Gray had evidently told him of
Allerick's condition. 'Mr Leigh!' he called,
and when the House-master reached the
dais he asked, 'Did you give Desmond a
pass?'

'No, sir,' answered Mr Leigh. 'He is
absent without permission.'

The Head-master frowned. 'That isn't
like Desmond. And it's awkward to-night,
of all nights. Well, thank you, Mr Leigh.

I shall deal with Desmond's offence when he returns.'

He called the roll and then conducted prayers, then, before dismissing the School, he said, 'You will all know by this time that B. D. Allerick is in the sanatorium suffering from an injury to the head which he received by falling this morning. It has caused his brain to become unbalanced. I hope there is no need to ask you to be as quiet as possible as you go along the passages, and to speak in low voices as you go along the balcony. Mrs Allerick is coming here to-night to see her son, and I will let you know how Allerick is after prayers in the morning. Good-night, boys.'

As he passed out of the hall he stopped Telford and asked, 'Do you know where Desmond has gone?'

'No, sir,' answered the Tiger. 'But perhaps D'Arcy will know.'

D'Arcy overheard, and could have strangled Telford at that moment for his helpful intentions.

'D'Arcy, do you know?' asked Dr Newton.

'Yes, sir; Desmond did tell me where he was going. He intended to be back at call-over, though, sir.'

'Where is he?'

'He asked me not to say, sir. He's not breaking rules or anything, and I know he really intended to be back for call-over. It won't be his fault if he's detained, sir.'

'I didn't ask you to act as Desmond's advocate, D'Arcy. You must learn to give a straightforward answer to a question. As you can't say where he has gone, you may go. Desmond must make his own explanation to me.'

His frown deepened as he went away, and D'Arcy looked troubled. 'I wish you'd shut up about it,' he said to the Tiger. 'The Newt'll think Des is doing something wrong.'

'Well, is he?'

'No, of course not, you ass!' snapped D'Arcy.

'Then why worry? Des'll be able to explain when he turns up.'

'Oh, go and eat coke, and don't interfere in things you don't understand,' was D'Arcy's pleasant retort as he turned away. The Tiger felt a passing twinge of jealousy. Why hadn't Desmond told him where he was going?

When Desmond had not returned by nine o'clock the Head sent for D'Arcy again. D'Arcy was pacing impatiently up and down before the School gates, looking down the

road, when the butler came for him. In a
very distressed frame of mind he hurried to
the Head's study.

'D'Arcy,' said the Head-master, 'you
must help me to find Desmond. Allerick
is getting dangerously restless, and asking
for him all the time. Where did Desmond
go? Surely, under the circumstances he
would not consider you were breaking his
confidence by telling me.'

D'Arcy fidgeted for a few moments, then
he replied, 'He went down to the village,
sir, to Dowling's shop.'

He hoped the Head-master would take it
for granted that Desmond had gone to make
a purchase, but his own expression gave Dr
Newton the clue.

'Why did he go there, D'Arcy?' questioned
the Head-master sternly.

'He—thought perhaps he could find out
more about—the theft—sir—he didn't mean
to be impertinent, but he thought perhaps—
Dowling knew more than he told you,' added
D'Arcy in a rush, 'and he was frightfully
worried about Allerick.'

Dr Newton gazed at the carpet for a few
moments, then he said abruptly, 'I see. Well,
it was impertinent, perhaps; but Desmond is
not impertinent, but only as conceited as most

youths. Thus far he was not breaking rules, but to remain out until after call-over, how do you explain that? You said he intended to return?'

'He did, sir.'

'Then something serious must have happened to prevent him. I will send Seddon to Dowling's to make inquiries. Six o'clock to nine is a long time to be away. I hope he isn't injured or something. Well, it's no use making gloomy premises. Go to bed, D'Arcy.'

'May Desmond call on me when he returns, sir?'

'No, certainly not; I'm not going to have you lying awake waiting for him. Desmond will account to me for his absence and then go straight to his own cubicle.'

But D'Arcy did not sleep, nor did the Head-master for that matter, for Seddon returned to say that Mr Dowling knew nothing whatever about Desmond, and nobody from the college had been in his shop that day. D'Arcy woke up at three, and the first thing he did was to climb upon his bed and look over the wooden division into Desmond's untidy cubicle. But the bed was empty still.

At seven o'clock the Head telephoned to the police, giving a description of Desmond.

He had hardly returned to his own study when there came a knock at the door and D'Arcy entered. The Head tried to smile. 'Well, D'Arcy, you're up early.'

'I couldn't wait to hear what has happened to Desmond, sir.'

'We don't know, D'Arcy. Don't look so worried, my boy; it is better than hearing he's been run over. I've telephoned to the police-station. One can't disappear completely in a small place like this, D'Arcy.'

D'Arcy looked as if he doubted the statement. 'But what about Dowling, sir?'

'It seems Desmond did not enter Mr Dowling's shop. On that point I am going to make further inquiries this morning. There is something about that man Dowling I do not like. But one mustn't let one's suspicions run riot.'

'How is Allerick, sir?' asked D'Arcy, and saw the Head's face cloud in spite of the cheerful tone in which he answered.

'Oh, not so ill as might be expected. Dr Gray was forced to give him a sleeping-mixture. Perhaps when he wakes up he will have lost his strange craving to speak to Desmond. All the same, I hope Desmond returns. It is most unfortunate that he should have disappeared just at this time. I am going to telegraph to his family now. There is just the slight possibility that he may have gone home. But I can't think of any reason for Desmond to run away from St Martin's, can you?'

'No, sir!' answered D'Arcy quite indignantly; 'he wouldn't do that.'

'Well, we'll soon know, I have no doubt. Don't worry, D'Arcy. And will you please tell Mr Leigh I am not able to conduct the Greek class this morning, and tell them to continue the translation of the *Bacchæ* from where we left off last lesson?'

'Yes, sir,' answered D'Arcy, going very slowly. He met Telford coming from the dormitory.

'Where's Des?' the Tiger shouted before he had reached D'Arcy.

'Don't ask me! He's vanished—dissolved into thin air!'

'Go hon!' the Tiger answered. 'Substantial animals like Des don't vanish. Don't pull my leg, Darkie; it's mean of you.'

'I am not pulling your leg, you idiot,' answered D'Arcy. 'Des has gone; the Newt's just been telephoning to the police and sending word to his people. I might just as well tell you, seeing I've told the Newt, that Des went to Dowling's last night. At least he

set out for there. Dowling says he didn't
turn up.'

'Whew!' gasped Telford. 'Where on earth
can he have got to! If he'd been injured
we'd have heard by this time surely. I say,
Darkie, Dowling's a queer stick—I wonder
if——'

'Oh, I've gone over all that ground about
sixty times!' snapped D'Arcy almost irritably.
'What could Dowling gain by telling lies?
And, short of kidnapping Des, he couldn't
do anything. Anyway, what use would it
be to kidnap old Des? His father's not
exactly a millionaire. I lay awake last night
puzzling over Dowling, but I got no further.
Have you got a prep first?'

'Yes.'

'Then let's go into the village and make
some inquiries. We can't do much, but it'll
all help. The police are on his track.'

'Righto. No use going to Dowling's,
though.'

'Oh, the Newt'll make sure Dowling's
looked after. We can ask at some of the
shops, though. It's a rotten affair. Desmond
always looks like a lord, and some rough
might have thought he was worth knocking
down.'

'Oh, he might knock him down,' answered

Telford, 'but he couldn't cause him to vanish from the middle of a village street—unless——'

'Oh, don't let's think about it,' said D'Arcy. 'Come and have brekker and we'll talk things over.'

After prayers the Head-master informed the School of Desmond's disappearance, said that he had not gone home, and did not appear to be in the village. A few inquiries produced the fact that Desmond was last seen by Black, who had noticed the captain of Leigh's swinging down the School-lane. The Head-master held a short conversation with Black, who said Desmond was obviously deep in thought, and in a great hurry.

'I shall expect everyone to do their best to find Desmond,' said Dr Newton. 'This seems to be a term of misadventures. Dismiss.'

He went straight from the hall to the sanatorium. Dr Gray was there, and decidedly more cheerful about Allerick. Allerick himself lay weakly back with closed eyes. His face against the white pillow appeared sallow almost to brownness.

'He's a lot better,' whispered Dr Gray to the Head-master. 'He's regained his memory and, except for being extremely excitable, he is almost normal. The cut has healed beautifully. Are you going to speak to him?'

'Is it all right?'

'Oh yes ; only I wouldn't speak of Desmond,' warned Dr Gray, 'unless he mentions him first, and then it would be better to answer as cheerfully as possible.'

'Very well,' said the Head-master, and walked over to the bed.

Allerick opened his eyes as though his eyelids were weighted and said, 'May I speak to Desmond now?'

CHAPTER XVI.

LORD INVERSLOWE.

THE Head-master answered very gently, 'Why do you want Desmond, Allerick?'

'I want to explain about something,' answered Allerick in a low weak voice. 'Was it this morning I knocked my head?'

'No; yesterday. You were asleep all yesterday.'

'Oh! Why does a bang on the head make a chap's limbs all wonky?'

'You were pretty run down, Allerick. I'm afraid this hasn't been a happy term for you.'

'In—one—way, it's the best I ever had,' Allerick answered dreamily. Then added persistently, 'Couldn't I speak to Desmond just for a minute, sir?'

'He's out,' Dr Newton said. 'And, anyway, you must keep quiet and not get excited. I'll send Desmond to you when I think you're fit to talk to him.'

'Thank you, sir, I'm all right—really. Des wouldn't be . . .' His voice trailed off into silence, and his eyes closed.

The Head went quietly away, to be met in the passage by Seddon. 'Inspector Smith waiting to see you, sir,' said the latter.

'Show him into my study,' said Dr Newton, his face paling a little. Would there be news of Desmond?

There was not.

'We've scoured the village, sir,' said the inspector. 'Nobody seems to know anything of the boy. I've just come to get particulars for a poster, if you don't mind.'

'Oh no; let's do everything we can,' answered the Head-master. 'Captain and Mrs Desmond must be most upset.'

Presently the inspector had drafted out the description of Desmond. 'There'll have to be a reward,' he said. 'Of course, we won't put this poster up just yet——'

'As soon as you like,' Dr Newton said. 'I'm assured of the fact that Desmond meant to return in time for call-over last night. I am afraid something terrible has happened. He is a splendid boy, and absolutely straight —he wouldn't run away. Offer a hundred pounds to begin with, and we can raise it if he doesn't turn up. I'll pay it myself.'

When Desmond was not discovered next day, notices were exhibited all around Calleridge and Lowesdale, which read:

· **A** reward of a hundred pounds will be paid for information leading to the discovery of the whereabouts of Neville Desmond, last seen in St Martin's School lane. Age 17, height 6 ft. ½ in., well built, with light brown hair, deep blue eyes, clear skin. Dressed in red and black St Martin's School cap and blazer, white cricket flannels, tan shoes. Any information should at once be given at Calleridge Police Station, or to Dr Newton, Headmaster, St Martin's School.'

This poster, together with a photograph of Desmond, became a subject of great interest in the village. Robson gazed at it for quite a long time, smiling as if it were most amusing. He knew Desmond was fastened in a dark cellar, that his father and mother were nearly frantic, that Dr Newton was pale with worry, that Allerick was getting no better, yet he smiled. Such was Robson's sense of humour. In School, however, he appeared as concerned as anyone else. 'Will you scratch the match against Cranfield?' he asked D'Arcy.

'Of course not,' said D'Arcy. 'We *can't* scratch the match. It's *the* match of the year.'

'I thought while Desmond——'

'I know as much about Des's play as you do!' snapped D'Arcy. 'He wouldn't want me to scratch if he was here.'

'Perhaps not, but——'

'And he'll probably be here by then, anyway.'

'Probably,' said Robson in a strange tone. D'Arcy gave him a piercing glance, but Robson's expression was quite inscrutable.

'We must all play up and make up for Des not being here,' said D'Arcy.

'Perhaps that won't be so very hard,' answered Robson; 'he didn't do so brilliantly in the last match.'

'Just like you to say a thing like that behind a chap's back!' retorted D'Arcy angrily. 'I suppose you feel bolder than a lion with Desmond away and Allerick in the san.'

'I prefer the cunning of the serpent to the boldness of the lion,' smiled Robson, apparently not at all taken aback by D'Arcy's outburst. 'One gets more excitement out of it.'

'Oh, you're mad!' said D'Arcy contemptuously, as he strode away. He was quite unable to take an interest in the match, which was planned for Saturday afternoon, but he knew he would have to go through with it. He had always been Desmond's chief chum, but never before had he realised how many of his interests in the School were bound up with those of Desmond. He found himself thinking, ' I must tell old Des,' and then realising that there was no ' Old Des ' to tell. And then the agony of not knowing whether Desmond were dead or alive ! Truly, it was hard to play even a cup-final inter-school cricket match under the circumstances. But they must not only play, they must win, for if they lost it would be the first time in ten years that the Grange Cup had left St Martin's. D'Arcy felt sure they would have won if Desmond had been on the scene with his queer curled balls that caused such havoc. Well, failing Desmond, there was Lestrange and himself—and Robson. Would Robson play as brilliantly as he had done in the match against Dale's ? Would he—when there was no Desmond to super-cede ? D'Arcy wondered, but did not care. What did the match matter with Desmond away ?

But worse things were in store. A shining saloon car drew up at the School door on the Thursday night. Lord Inverslowe, stout and solemn, alighted from it and informed Seddon that he wished to speak to the Head-master. Dr Newton was conducting the call-over, but when he heard that the matter was urgent he asked Mr Wright to finish the register, and strode along to his study.

Lord Inverslowe had ensconced himself there in the deep arm-chair, and was mopping his red perspiring face with a huge silk handkerchief. 'Well, Tony,' he said, struggling to his feet as Dr Newton entered. 'I've come all the way from London since lunch, and I'm dead beat. But what's up, old man? You look about sixty.'

'The captain of Leigh's House—Desmond—has disappeared, that's all,' answered the Head. 'We can't trace him. He's been gone since Tuesday evening.'

Lord Inverslowe stared hard at the Head, the news appeared to effect him deeply. 'What sort of a boy was he?'

'A splendid young chap,' the Head said. 'But why have you paid me this unexpected visit, Harry? I thought you were going to France.'

'So I was, till—I say, Tony, I've got something rather dreadful to tell you.'

The Head winced. 'The times are rather trying,' he said. 'One trouble on top of another—the medallion—Desmond, and now——?'

'But this is still the medallion,' Lord Inverslowe broke in, placing his chubby hand on his friend's shoulder. 'Oh, dash it, I know you'll be awfully cut up!' he groaned quite boyishly.

'But you've got your medallion back all right!' the Head said in bewilderment. 'What do you mean? If it's been stolen again, you deserve it, that's all,' he added quite sternly.

Lord Inverslowe smiled ruefully and shook his head. 'No, Tony, it's not stolen again. It was never returned.'

The Head gazed at him, unable to grasp his meaning. The other thrust his hand into his vest-pocket and drew out a jewel-case. Snapping this open, he held out the medallion within it.

'But that's the Necra medallion,' said Dr Newton.

'Look again!' answered Lord Inverslowe quietly.

The Head studied the medallion carefully, then looked up in his friend's face. 'What do you mean? Isn't this the same one? Are there two?'

'No,' replied Lord Inverslowe, shaking the medallion contemptuously. 'There is only one Necra medallion, and this is not it. It is still in the hands of the thief who stole it that afternoon.'

The Head sank into a chair and leant his head on his hands. 'Oh, this is about the last straw, Harry,' muttered he. 'I thought, at least, though the mystery of its theft wasn't cleared up, you'd got the thing back. Here's another mystery to supplement that of Desmond's disappearance.'

A gleam lit Lord Inverslowe's bead-like eyes for a second. 'Do you think,' he suggested tentatively, 'that the two affairs could have any connection with each other?'

Dr Newton raised his head, and his eyes were almost angry. 'I'm certain they couldn't,' he snapped. 'No. Put that out of your head. Desmond is as far from being a thief as Allerick—farther, if possible.'

'We are not dealing with a crude school-boy thief,' the other persisted. 'Whoever stole the Necra medallion and had a fake made is a jolly clever thief, and such a rogue would be able to dissimulate pretty well——'

'There's no dissimulation about Desmond,' interrupted Dr Newton. 'He looks what he is—and that's not a thief.'

'Oh well, you know best, I suppose, Tony. It's all pretty rotten. What about the other boy—Allerick?'

'He's in the sanatorium—ill,' replied the Head. 'No, it couldn't have been Allerick, either; it's obviously someone much cleverer and craftier than either of those two boys. Look here, Harry,' went on he, with a sudden inspiration, 'are you sure it was the real medallion you had on the library table?'

'Certain. There was one ruby in the real medallion much darker than the others. I pointed it out to the boy who asked me the question about it. This—fake has no darker ruby.'

'Well, that's no clue, then,' sighed the Head. 'I give up, Harry. I suppose— you'd better bring the police into it— now. . .' He tried to speak unaffectedly, but suddenly his voice went quite hoarse. St Martin's meant so much to him. He was young and enthusiastic, and wanted the School to be perfect.

Lord Inverslowe was silent. He gazed down at his friend's shining dark head, at his firm cleft chin on which the scar showed quite clearly to-day. 'What do you think, Tony?' he asked quietly.

The Head raised his blue eyes. 'You must get your medallion, Harry,' he said. 'Theft is theft—but—you know how I—I mean—the School is . . .' He could get no

farther, and bent his head again so that
Lord Inverslowe could not read his expression.
But he felt the grip of the other's hand
on his shoulder again, and looked up at
last to see Lord Inverslowe smiling.

'Tony, you silly ass. You've made a little
tin god of the School. It would half-kill
you if it was branded with theft.'

'Yes,' said the Head ; 'I deserve it. I've
thought too much of the School's honour,
and——'

'No, I don't mean that—I don't intend
it ever to be so branded if I can help it,
Tony. Isn't the School more important than
my collection ? I only collect relics of the
dead past, you treasure specimens of the
present youth. *They* must be considered,
and *their* love of the school . . .'

As the Head-master looked up in bewilderment at him Lord Inverslowe laughed, and
ended : 'Stupid old thing, do you think I've
forgotten Ellingford—or Cambridge—or Gallipoli, Tony ? Gallipoli, and the mud and flies
and the glory that we shared there ? Why,
man, your jolly old peace of mind is more
to me than fifty Necra medallions. Blow
the police——'

'But—the loss ? ' stammered the Head,
though hope was glowing in his eyes again.

'Oh, blow the loss! What's fifty thousand? Buck up, Tony, and look your age. You're not a hundred, you know—you're thirty-six, old bean! We must try to find this boy, Desmond——'

'Harry, how can I thank you——' began Dr Newton.

'Shut up!' interrupted Lord Inverslowe almost fiercely. 'Ring the bell and get your butler Johnny to bring me a substantial meal and some port. Didn't I tell you I'd been travelling since lunch? 'Pon my word, Tony, you never bother yourself about a chap's personal welfare.' He sank into the arm-chair again. 'As for that,' he ended, throwing the jewel-case carelessly on to the desk, 'give it to some kid to play with.'

CHAPTER XVII.

HERO OF THE HOUR.

SATURDAY was an ideal day for cricket, warm and yet fresh, sunny without being dazzling, but D'Arcy sighed heavily as he changed into his flannels. Some strange optimism suggested to him that even now Desmond might arrive mysteriously in time for the match, and he spread out on a chair the large shirt, trousers, leg-guards, and bat belonging to his friend.

Telford came in at two o'clock and gazed at these. 'What are these for, Darkie?'

'I—just—thought——'

Telford shook his head slowly. 'It's no go, old man,' he said; 'there'll be no Desmond at this match.'

D'Arcy's face was almost haggard, and the mischievous gleam had quite vanished from his eyes. The rest of the School might go on almost as usual without Desmond, but not D'Arcy. Desmond's influence was stronger upon him than upon anyone else. Some people were even beginning to believe that

Desmond had run away to sea (of course, it is quite usual to go to sea in a cap and blazer); others even hinted that it was strange that his disappearance should occur just about the time when the medallion was discovered to be a fake, for, in spite of Lord Inverslowe's efforts to keep this latter fact a secret, it was all over the School by Saturday. D'Arcy had fought seven people during that short time for merely looking dubious when Desmond's name was mentioned; but now the bad opinion was so prevalent that it was impossible to deal with all offenders, and D'Arcy had relapsed into silent disgust. He was sitting dressed, ready to go on the field when the Cranfield team should arrive, when there was a knock at the door. 'Come in!' he called, without looking up.

'I want you, D'Arcy,' said Dr Gray, as he came in. 'Allerick is much better, and insists upon coming down for the match. The Head-master's just told him about Desmond.'

'Oh!' D'Arcy rose, stretching himself. 'What did he say?'

'He's most strange about it. I don't think he half-believes it, somehow. Well, come and help me to get him down, will you?'

'Why don't you ask O'Shane?'

'He's busy dressing—and besides you're stronger. Come on, don't be so lazy. This is most strange about Desmond,' said the doctor, as they mounted the stairs together. 'I can't believe the boy would run away— yet if he had been kidnapped, the kidnappers would have sent in their terms to Captain Desmond before now.'

'It's not Desmond's fault, anyway,' answered D'Arcy. 'Oh, we wish we *knew* where he was —I—he——' He broke off, irritable and confused.

The doctor placed his hand on the boy's shoulder. 'Don't let yourself get like that, anyway,' he said. 'Play up, D'Arcy, as Desmond would if you'd gone. Besides, remember Allerick. You *must* be as cheerful as you can with him.'

D'Arcy had no chance to answer, because at that moment they reached the sanatorium. Allerick was reclining in a long chair by the window. It was astonishing how those few days had altered him. He had always been thin, now he was almost cadaverous; his eyes appeared too large for his head. As soon as he saw D'Arcy he said, 'Hullo, D'Arcy! What's this about Desmond? He hasn't run away, has he?'

'No,' answered D'Arcy; 'I think he's been shanghaied or something. He went out on Tuesday and didn't come back.'

'What? Where did he go to?'

D'Arcy hesitated for a minute, then he said, 'He went down to the village, as a matter of fact—to Dowling's.'

'What?' Allerick's start caused Dr Gray to approach him warningly. 'Why?'

'He'd got some bee in his bonnet about getting further partics—about, you know what. He asked me not to tell anyone; but I had to tell the Head and the Tiger, so I might as well tell you.'

'Well, hasn't Dowling anything to do with it?'

'Come along, and I'll explain as we go,' answered D'Arcy.

They carried Allerick, still in the long chair, down the stairs into the field as D'Arcy told him the whole story. Allerick didn't say much, but his eyes seemed to burn as D'Arcy looked at him.

'What a term!' Allerick breathed.

'I never saw one like it!' agreed D'Arcy. 'There's the Cranfieldians. I never felt less like cricket in my life.'

The Cranfield team was a splendid one, and last year St Martin's had only just

beaten them.   D'Arcy, covertly studying
Pilling, their little thin captain who sent the
stinging twisted balls, and Randle, their
almost infallible batsman, wondered if these
two could not beat a St Martin's team that
contained no Desmond.

After an hour's play he was still more
anxious about results.   There was something
lacking in St Martin's play, there seemed to
be no life in it, whereas the Cranfield team
were swift and eager.   With St Martin's
second innings, the anxiety increased.   The
spectators who crowded the benches and the
grass mound round the field began to consider things were hopeless.   They saw the
cup being ruthlessly dragged from its ten
years' standing and carried away by the
cheering Cranfield men.   The play went
slower and slower, the Cranfield score loomed
far beyond that of St Martin's.   D'Arcy was
bowled out for nine.

Then Robson went in to bat.   He walked
to the wicket with a half-smile upon his
handsome face, nonchalantly, easily, as though
he were strolling aimlessly across the field.
He was perfectly clad, spotless, and held
himself like a king.   A little thrill went
round the Cranfield men at the sight of
him, and there are scores in St Martin's

who remember Robson as he appeared then as clearly as if their minds had made an unfading photograph of him.

And he saved the match. Desmond, D'Arcy, and all the rest of the St Martin's team, even Telford, who was opposite Robson, were forgotten. Robson played as he had never played before. The ball flashed like a red bird as it flew through the shining air. The St Martin's score mounted and mounted. Robson seemed gifted with the power of foreseeing the intention of the bowler. Even Pilling could not trap him.

He not only saved the match, but St Martin's won more gloriously than the year before. Cranfield had nothing but admiration for Robson—and as for St Martin's, words could not describe their joy. They shouldered Robson, they hurrahed, they cheered, they carried him, shoulder high, in triumph to Wright's common-room, and the sound in there made a bedlam of the whole School.

Only a few fellows did not join in the excitement. When the Cranfield team had gone, D'Arcy rejoined Allerick, Hare, and O'Shane, and even the result of the match had not made his expression any happier.

'Robson played wonderfully,' said Hare,

who had been caught out with sixteen to his score. 'Jolly fine.'

'We should be there congratulating him,' O'Shane murmured; 'but somehow I can't bring myself to do it. It may not be sporting—but——'

'Why should we like him any more because he won the match?' growled D'Arcy. 'Dash it, there's plenty of people to make a little tin god of him without us! And if Des had been here,' he ended savagely, 'the match would have been ours in any case.'

'I dare say,' answered Allerick. He could not rid his mind of the shining portrait of Robson at the wicket. 'I give Robson up. I can't understand him. He's a perfect rotter, and yet—who, not knowing what we do, could fail to admire him this afternoon?'

No one apparently. Robson was the hero of the hour. He was toasted and sung, his name was on everyone's lips, his words were listened to as an oracle. The most wonderful thing was that, in the excitement, quite half of Leigh's House crowded into Wright's to surround the great man.

D'Arcy gave a bitter little smile, as, after helping Allerick back to the sanatorium, he strode along Leigh's empty corridors. Here was the thing Desmond had struggled to

obtain—Leigh's and Wright's united by a
common bond of sportsmanship and school
triumph; and Robson—Robson had brought
it to pass. 'Come and have tea with the
Tiger and me,' he said to O'Shane and Hare
when they showed signs of departing.

'I'd be only too glad,' answered O'Shane
for the two of them. 'I don't know why
Dr Gray won't let us take tea up to Rix in
the san. Still, one can't disobey the doctor,
can one?'

'One can't,' retorted D'Arcy. 'Come on,
then.'

When they entered the study he went
immediately to the chair, and, folding up
Desmond's cricket-flannels, put them away
again. There was a curious flush on his
face as he did so. He was a long time
placing the leg-pads in the cupboard, and
the other two stood gazing out of the
window in unhappy silence. O'Shane was
thinking of Allerick up there in the san
alone. Hare, in the depths of his clever
mind, was considering still the strange
problem of Robson—puzzling over him.
And D'Arcy was wondering if ever again
he would see Desmond strapping those pads
on to his huge legs—laughing—punching
his study-mate if he disagreed with him. . . .

So it was not a very happy party that the Tiger discovered when he came in, carrying bags of sausage-rolls and buns. 'Might as well have a bit of a beano,' he explained, 'as we're not honouring the one at which our dear friend Robbie is presiding. Do you know,' he added, 'I may be awfully unsporting, but I hate the fellow worse than ever now. There's something uncanny about a chap who can play as he did this afternoon after the way he conducted that beastly boxing match with Rix. It's not done. It's not square. I think I'd rather we'd lost the match.'

O'Shane and Hare gasped; but D'Arcy answered, 'Tiger, I give you points; you're pluckier than I am. I guess I've been thinking that all along, only I hadn't the nerve to say it. I don't think I wanted the School to win, really, when Des wasn't there——'

'But the Cranfield chaps don't know that Robson's such a rotter, you know,' broke in O'Shane, 'so we're not exactly let down in any way. And Desmond'll be jolly glad we won, you know, though he wasn't there. Besides, that boxing-match business was perhaps an accident after all——'

'Oh, you're too Christian, Pat!' said Telford.

'I didn't see Robson trip Rix up, but I'll bet he did. And Desmond saw him. A chap doesn't trip another up by accident. And if it was an accident, Robson would have owned up to it and apologised. But he swore everyone out his foot was nowhere near Rix's.'

'Oh, he's a rotter right enough!' D'Arcy said; 'but we might as well have tea.'

Meanwhile the 'rotter' was enjoying himself immensely. He was very quiet, merely smiling when any specially exaggerated praise was offered him, but the gleam in his grey eyes told of his contempt for the wild crowd. As the evening wore on, however, he spoke more, and even told some funny stories which made the others roar with laughter whether they saw the point or not. Finally they toasted him in lemonade.

'Robson, the best fellow yet!' shouted Gregory, as they clinked glasses; then they sang, 'For he's a jolly good fellow,' and 'The more we are together.'

After that the merry crowd began to dwindle, slipping away in little groups, until there were some twenty fellows left, all of whom belonged to Wright's House.'

'Getting late!' said Spencer at last, with a yawn. 'But, I say, Robbie, what about those snaps you said you'd show us? You know, of the yacht and all that?'

'Oh, I forgot about them, old man,' said Robson; 'I'll go and get them. I won't be a sec.'

'Shall I come?' asked Gregory eagerly.

'Oh, don't bother,' answered Robson easily, 'I know exactly where they are. Clear a space on the table, then I can spread them out, don't you know.' He turned in the doorway, smiling, and it seemed as if he were posing before them.

Gregory, who by now worshipped the ground Robson walked on, never forgot him as he stood there—the electric light making his fair hair gleam like an aureole—his white figure outlined so clearly against the darkness of the passage.

'I sha'n't be a sec!' he said again, and walked along the passage to his study.

Arrived there his procedure was strange indeed. He locked the door, and with astounding rapidity he changed into a dark navy-blue suit and overcoat, and a turned-down Trilby hat. From behind his curtain he drew out a large brown Gladstone bag. He crossed to the mirror and gazed for a moment at his reflection, smiling at the change. Instead of a care-free boy he now looked a man, excited and out for adventure. Quietly he opened the window, and after glancing round the field to make sure there was no one watching, he climbed over the sill, and, running lightly across the field, slipped through a gap in the hedge and along the road.

Meanwhile the crowd in the common-room had grown impatient.

'Old Robbie's taking a frightfully long time!' said Spencer. 'Shall we go and hurry him up?'

'Righto,' said Gregory. 'Come on,' and the two strolled along the passage to Robson's study.

'Hurry up, Rob!' called Gregory. There was no answer. He turned the handle to open the door. 'The door's locked!' he exclaimed. 'I say, Robbie, it's us!' he shouted inanely.

No answer.

'Whatever's happened?' exclaimed Spencer, and it seemed to him suddenly as if they had waited for quite a long time to go after Robson, only to find his door locked and his room empty. It was almost as if, somehow, Robson, the dauntless hero, had been too good to be true.

'Nothing, you ass,' answered Gregory.

'He can't hear us, that's all. Come round to the window through Cairns's study.'

They entered the next study and, climbing through the window, went round to Robson's study and gazed in. The room was empty, and in the centre of the floor lay Robson's beautiful cricket-flannels, cast there like a piece of old rag. Gregory's face went as white as a sheet.

'Whatever's happened?' was all that Spencer could mumble.

'You fool, you've said that once!' answered Gregory, without knowing what he said. 'Rob! Rob! Rob!'

The empty room seemed to mock him. The wind blew into the room and stirred the curtains in the corner. Gregory saw it and his expression changed. 'He's hiding!' he laughed. 'Look, I saw him . . .' He sprang into the room and pulled the curtains aside, chuckling. An empty corner greeted him. For a moment he stood still, unable to grasp matters, then he seemed to calm down, his surprise turned to despair. He turned round to Spencer and said quietly, 'Rob's gone!'

'But why? Why?' queried Spencer hopelessly. 'Oh, it's just a silly joke—it can't be anything else!'

Gregory kicked the cricket-flannels aside

almost angrily. 'It's a rotten trick,' he said, as if trying to reassure himself; 'and I'll jolly well tell him so, too, the next time I see him.'

But he did not have the chance, for he never saw Robson again.

CHAPTER XVIII.

DESMOND RETURNS.

ROBSON went straight down to Dowling's. The shop was closed, but when he had given a sharp triple knock at the side-door Dowling admitted him. 'You're early!' he said, as he switched on the light in the crowded sitting-room.

Robson sat on the table and removed the big hat from his fair head. 'I had to come when I got the chance,' he answered. 'I have an eye for effect, and flatter myself that I've given that School two really good thrills to-day. The thrill of my play this afternoon won't be half so good as that of discovering that the wondrous nightingale has flown its golden cage.' He laughed as happily and boyishly as Desmond might have done.

Dowling studied him a little nervously. 'I—hope everything's safe?' he questioned, his bird-like eyes darting backwards and forwards over the room.

'Quite safe,' Robson assured him; 'but

also quite dramatic.' He slipped from the table and became suddenly very business-like. 'Well—got the money?' he flung out.

Dowling shook his head slowly. Robson frowned.

'I tried seven more places,' Dowling told him. 'It's no use.'

'You should have let me know,' Robson snapped in great annoyance. 'I could have stayed at St Martin's a bit longer. I was doing well there—quite a tin god in my own way. I was enjoying it. I'd not have left if I'd known you wouldn't have the money ready.'

'I couldn't help it,' answered the other querulously. 'I did my best. The only thing you can do is to palm off the rubies, one by one, that's all. If you remember, I said it was too big a proposition at the first.' He seemed a little afraid of Robson, who was glowering angrily in his disappointment.

'Oh well,' said the boy at last, 'give me the medallion. I can't stay now, anyway. How's our friend in the cellar?'

'Ay, that's another thing,' Dowling said. 'It's time he was let out. He's none too chirpy. I don't want no corpses lying about below my house.'

Robson's frown deepened. 'Don't be mad,'

he answered. 'Here, I'll go in and see him. You can let him out to-night. I'll have sailed by that time, and there won't be any fear of what he might say. Get me a candle. But—no—the medallion first, please.'

Dowling opened the drawer in the side-board and took out a wash-leather bag. With some reluctance he handed this to Robson.

Robson opened the bag and studied the medallion which lay within, wrapped in dirty cotton-wool. 'It's a lovely thing,' he murmured, as he slipped it into his overcoat-pocket. 'I'll be sorry to pull it to pieces. But cruel necessity demands it. Now for Desmond!'

They went into the kitchen, and Dowling drew up the trap-door while Robson lighted the candle. A smell of damp unwholesome walls came up from the cellar, and Robson's delicate nostrils quivered in disgust. 'Pah—what a hole!' he breathed. 'I don't think even Desmond deserved this.'

'Where else could I put him?' asked Dowling. 'The place was searched by the police, anyway, in vain. A jolly good hiding-place, this is. They say a whole hoard of Jacobites were stored here and escaped.'

'A yarn,' retorted Robson. 'The place isn't old enough.'

He climbed carefully down the rotting ladder, and held up the flickering candle. There was no sound, but as he moved forward he almost fell over a pair of legs, and lowering the candle he saw Desmond lying there, asleep. Flat on the dirty stones he lay— the boy who had been used to a feather-mattress all his life. His blazer was crumpled and torn, and his flannels stained with green and brown mould from the walls. His wrists were cut and reddened with the rope around them, and there was dust in his rough hair and on his pale cheeks. Robson gazed at him for quite a long time without remorse, in fact, almost as though the sight gave him satisfaction. Then he stepped down and shook Desmond roughly.

Desmond's eyelids fluttered, then he awoke, suddenly and cruelly from the comfort of his dreams to the misery of the cold cellar.

Robson saw hope and then despair in the sea-blue eyes that met his, then he said lightly, 'I came to make sure you were quite well and happy in your temporary residence, Desmond. I'm glad you've enjoyed your stay here. I feel sure you will be sorry that it terminates to-night.'

Desmond's lips tightened; he merely gazed at Robson without speaking.

Robson had a sudden desire to goad his enemy to fury, to see him wild with anger and unable to relieve his feelings. 'You are a fool, Desmond,' he said. 'What is more, a fool convinced of his own astuteness. No one but you would have discussed private plans in front of a shrubbery which afforded a splendid hiding-place. And having done so, no one but you would have walked so gaily into the lion's den.'

Desmond did not move; indeed, he seemed scarcely to hear.

'It is also a pity about that other feeble idiot, Allerick,' went on Robson. 'I grew quite tired of hearing Dr Gray say Allerick continued to ask for you, and that if you weren't discovered the results would be serious . . .' He saw Desmond's face twitch, then the bright colour rushed into his face. 'I was quite sorry for Allerick——'

'What do you mean? What's the matter with Allerick?' burst out Desmond.

Robson shrugged his broad shoulders, half-smiling. 'No concern of mine,' he murmured. 'Still——'

Desmond made a desperate effort to strike Robson with his bound fists, but Robson, expecting the move, sprang quickly back.

'Better not be *too* energetic, Desmond,'

said he, 'or I might tell Mr Dowling that
it would be better for you if you remained
in the pleasant underground palace for a
month or so. It wouldn't make any difference
to me, you know. By the time you get
back to the pining and quite mentally-deficient
Allerick I'll be far, far away—in a happier,
better place than this; a place which will re-
cognise my wonderful genius, assisted always,
of course, by the Necra medallion.' He
paused. Desmond, after that futile attempt
to strike his tormentor, had lain back again
with closed eyes.

'But in case the dear Newt should make
inquiries about the pleasant conversation we're
having,' went on Robson, 'I will endeavour
to give you a little more information. It
begins with chewing-gum. You have heard
of chewing-gum, no doubt—a very plebeian
and American edible, but useful, Desmond,
quite useful, especially in its latter and more
plastic stages. For instance, it is quite handy,
and only needs to be assisted by a little
sleight-of-hand to transfer fifty thousand
pounds' worth of rubies from the upper side of
the table to the under one. This trick is most
amusing, and quite exciting too, when people
begin to search under the table and through
the pockets of the gentleman who performs

it. Also, it is pleasant to return to the
scene of battle, as it were, and to find the
little cache still laid up against a rainy day.
I'd try it, Desmond, really I would. Mr
Dowling's friend would be only too glad, on
the payment of a small sum, to make adequate
fakes of any small objects you might remove
in this manner, and—there is always Allerick's
desk — or perhaps even D'Arcy's . . .' He
stopped, because Desmond still did not appear
to be listening.

'Another good idea,' he went on, 'is to
put an additional ingredient into a glass of
lemonade—very interesting, especially if one
rescues from drowning the unlucky person
who happened to drink it.'

There was a moment's silence, then
Desmond suddenly opened his eyes and sat
up. 'I'm sorry for you, Robson,' he said.
'It's such a pity you're not straight. You're
so clever.'

'Straight!' Robson was stung, and laughed
to hide the fact. 'Bah! Only futile idiots
like you stick up for a code of rules and
spend their lives arguing over them. Thank
goodness I'm cast in a different mould. I've
been captain of a House, and that's all the
rotten St Martin's was worth to me. If I
could have had Loring's place I'd have been

content to stay there as a kind of uncrowned
king. I'd have altered the place considerably. But I'm going to have adventure
and life and excitement, not a wishy-washy
existence like yours.'

'That's the point,' answered Desmond.
'That's why I'm sorry for you; you don't
know what life and excitement and adventure
mean——'

'Pah!' broke in Robson. 'What do you
think you are—a suffering martyr? I can
see you playing the handsome hero to perfection when you get back to St Martin's.
And you can tell them from me, Desmond,
that there are other people besides Allerick
who believe in Communism, among them
being the gentleman who was kind enough to
bring me up according to his own principles.
Unlike Allerick, however, he does not merely
talk largely at debates, but applies his theory
of the division of wealth. Of course, the
division may sometimes be uneven—the
cleverer people getting a larger share—containing baubles like the Necra medallion.'

'Do you mean you were adopted by a
jewel-thief?' asked Desmond, and if ever he
pitied Robson it was at this revelation.

Robson laughed. 'A Communist, my dear
Desmond. He is cleverer than either you

or Allerick will ever be, and I respond
perfectly to his teaching. You see, I am
eternally grateful to him for rescuing me
from an orphanage almost as tediously bound
to tradition as St Martin's. Certainly I did
not think I should get such a splendid
opportunity to prove my ability. St Martin's
was to be merely a rest for recuperation
before starting bigger things, but—well, Lord
Inverslowe is fat and red, what does he
want with the Necra medallion? It was
sheer luck. There's a lot in luck, Desmond,
and yours is out this time, my friend. But
you're a noble hero from this time on, so
you have your reward. Bravo, Desmond,
bravo. And farewell. *You'll* be forgotten
as soon as you leave the School, but I
flatter myself they won't forget *me* in a
hurry.'

‘What a poor boast!’ answered Desmond;
‘and anyone could pinch a medallion.’

‘Try it and see how easy it is!’ Robson
said. ‘And as for remembering, well, here's
my last souvenir to you.’ He drew back,
and then, making a swift movement forward,
smacked Desmond's cheek with all his might.

Desmond fell backwards, his head coming
sharply against the floor. He murmured
weakly, ‘And anyone could hit a chap

whose hands were tied. Yes, I'll remember you, Robson, as the supreme example of an unmitigated cad.'

'That's very satisfactory, then,' laughed Robson. 'Farewell, Desmond. Give my kind regards to Dr Newton, and tell Gregory I was sorry to leave so suddenly, but I had an urgent summons.' He gave a last glance at Desmond's still form, then turned and, holding the candle above him so that its light illumined his fair hair, mounted the creaking ladder and disappeared.

Weak and aching, Desmond lay there for a few minutes, then he stretched out his bound hands and crawled over the floor to the place where Robson had stood when he struck him. Presently Desmond laughed, laughed as he had never laughed before, then he sank back again on the rough tiles and dozed into a miserable and nightmare-haunted sleep.

About six hours later he was awakened for the second time, but this time it was Dowling who bent over him. The old man was heavily dressed for a journey, and carried a bag. Behind him stood a huge—or he appeared huge in the semi-darkness—man, with a thick black beard, sun-tanned skin, and black shining eyes. Some sort of

foreigner, Desmond decided, wondering if
this were fact or but another nightmare.
But he was soon decided. Dowling cut the
ropes which bound his arms, and then,
motioning to the stranger, he dragged the
boy to his feet. The big man moved forward and grasped Desmond's shoulders with
fingers that seemed to grip the flesh like
iron clamps.

Desmond became suddenly wide - awake,
but it was the terrible intent wakefulness
of a person in danger. The severing of his
bonds had given him a new courage, and
his fearless blue eyes, sunk low, met the
black ones of the foreigner steadily.

'You'll be all right if you behave,' the
latter informed him. 'Quite all right. But
you scream or try to get away, and you'll
discover that sometimes very unpleasant
things can happen in country lanes. We're
going to set you free, all in good time, so
you be sensible and do as we say.' His
voice was thick and unpleasant, and Desmond remembered long afterwards the sound
of it breaking through the gloom.

Then Dowling and the stranger came one
on each side of him, and half-led, half-dragged
him up the stairs to the kitchen. It seemed
to Desmond that his legs did not belong to

him and were moving along of their own
accord, yet his brain was wonderfully alert,
and he noticed the dismantled state of the
room and the bareness of the passage that
was so crowded when he first saw it. He
wondered if the theft of the Necra medallion
was the cause of Dowling's flight. Of
course, he could not stay and be imprisoned
for kidnapping, but Desmond wondered if
the shop had always been receiving stolen
goods.

When they came out in the moonlit road,
and the night wind blew over his hair
and cooled his cheeks, Desmond could have
screamed with relief. He felt as though he
had never known till now what it was to
breathe. Forgetting his two strange companions, he drew long deep breaths, involuntarily his shoulders straightened and
his head went up. The dark-bearded man
watched him curiously, appraising the boy's
fine straight limbs and broad chest.

Outside was a small motor, an old and
very battered Ford. As the two men
pushed Desmond into this the captain of
Leigh's found himself remembering various
films in which the young and handsome
earl had been bundled away in just such a
manner. A little thrill of excitement went

through him. Something to tell Darkie.
Then the thought that perhaps he would
never again see D'Arcy steadied him. Living
on bread and water for days in a dark cellar
does not make for coherent thinking, but
Desmond knew that there was no chance
of escape. He could not see where they
were going, but could feel that the car was
rushing downhill, which meant that they
were travelling away from St Martin's, for
the School was on the summit of Pax Hill.

They had not travelled long, twenty
minutes at the most, before the motor
stopped, and the driver said, 'Netherlowe
Woods. Is this far enough?'

'Oh, quite,' answered Dowling. 'Come
on, Rogerson.'

They dragged Desmond out, and leaving
him standing bewildered in the middle of
the road, started the motor again and were
gone.

Desmond could hardly realise his freedom.
He stood there, half expecting the motor
to return and take him prisoner again. But
the car was travelling so fast that in a few
minutes he could not hear it. Absolute
silence wrapped him in, and almost total
darkness. Then a bird called from above
and the trees rustled, and he realised that

he was at the entrance to the woods which
had been the scene of many a youthful ramble
from St Martin's. Desmond shivered suddenly, and realised his dreadful weariness.
The clearness of brain had gone from him
and his eyes were heavy with sleep, every
limb of his body was aching. He walked
on till he felt the rough friendly trunk of a
great tree and the long grass around his
legs, then he cast himself down there, as
though it were the safest bedroom in the
world, and slept—slept as he had never
before slept in his life, and there was no
Robson or Dowling to waken him now.

When he awoke he found the place bathed
in silver morning light and the birds already
singing their welcome to the day. Desmond
opened his sunken Viking eyes and was
filled with wonder at the beauty of the scene
around him. He could not have chosen a
more lovely place in which to rest. Beside
him was a round pool of bright water,
surrounded by long grass among which were
bright campion and forget-me-nots, and above
it pale willows danced and flickered. Desmond
drew a long deep breath of sheer joy. After
that cellar this place was heaven. In a few
minutes his clothes lay below the tree and
he was leaving all the dust and grime of the

prison below the sparkling water. Then he
stood there, straight and strong, stretching
his muscular arms above his head; his hair
dripped silver drops, the colour had returned
to his cheeks, and his eyes were bright again.

He dressed, made for the road, and
strode briskly along, filled with uncontrollable
excitement. He wondered what had happened at the School; how they had taken
his disappearance. Where was Robson, and
would they ever find him again? At
the thought of Robson, Desmond laughed.
He became aware of the fact that he was
very hungry, and it was more than fifteen
miles to the School. He must eat, and soon.
After all he had been away from the School
for days, and an hour or two could not
make much difference. As soon as he reached
a cottage he asked for a breakfast, giving
his name and promising double repayment
when he reached the School. After a meal
of bacon and eggs and strong fresh tea he
felt decidedly better, and he was whistling
as he set off again. He passed a telephone-
box, and was about to use it when he
realised he had no twopence to pay for the
call. No, he could not soften the shock of
his return that way.

Quite the most interesting moment of

that walk home was that one when he came upon the poster describing the missing 'Neville Desmond.' He gazed at it with great interest, discovering for the first time that he was 'well-built.' So his eyes were deep blue, were they—and not green? Well, that was something to know.

When he reached the bottom of Pax Hill and saw the School he could have cried aloud for joy.

He was a strange figure as he marched through the quiet morning streets in his torn and stained blazer. He had lost his cap, and his hair was the extreme of untidyness. By the time he reached the School gates he was very tired, and his feet, in the golf-shoes that were not made for a dusty road, were very sore.

There were two or three fellows strolling round the field. It would be third lesson, and they should be doing prep. No, what day was it? The church bells answered his question. It was Sunday—Sunday morning.

Suddenly a burst of sunshine lit the whole scene, and Desmond felt extraordinarily happy. He stood looking—looking at the School; then he heard behind him the queer, almost choked, cry, 'Des! Des!' and, looking round, he saw D'Arcy.

'Darkie!' They had clasped hands and were laughing in sheer relief.

'Des! Oh—I say—where have you been, you rotter?'

'It's a long tale . . .' Desmond stared around him, then back at D'Arcy, his flush like a red wave over his face. 'Oh—it's good to be back! I say—Darkie—where's Rix?'

CHAPTER XIX.

THE END OF THE FEUD.

THE Head-master leaned his head on his hands; he was deeply interested. 'Yes —go on, Desmond,' he murmured.

'Then—he bent down again, sir, and this fell out of his pocket . . .' Desmond did not tell the Head about Robson slapping his face, not because of any false sentiment he possessed now about telling the worst of Robson, but because of his own pride, which still could not bear the thought of that insult.

There was a gleam in his eyes as he held out the leather bag to the Head-master, and a strange silence fell when it was opened. The dirty cotton-wool being removed, there lay on the desk the true, the one and only Necra medallion, flashing with unquenchable red fire.

The Head-master did not exclaim as he did when Robson had handed him the faked medallion. Somehow, since twelve o'clock, when on his way from the chapel he met the ragged but glowing captain of Leigh's, he felt that nothing could surprise him again.

'You mean to say, Desmond,' he said, 'that after all the plotting and planning and dishonesty that has gone on around this thing that it has fallen from Robson's hands into yours by a simple accident?'

'Yes, sir!' smiled Desmond; then, his smile fading and a rapid flush taking its place, 'Don't you believe me, sir?'

'Of course,' answered Dr Newton. 'By now,' he added, without meaning any offence, 'I think I'd believe anything.'

'Well, that's all, sir, except that they took me to Netherlowe Woods and left me there. I slept there, and then walked back!'

'Walked back! But it's a good sixteen miles!'

'Yes, sir—about that.' Desmond surveyed his dusty shoes ruefully. 'And it's fine to be back.'

'I'm sure. But, dear me, I forgot how hungry you must be in the interest of your story. You must have a good big Sunday dinner. I'll go now and let your parents know.'

Desmond whistled like a bird while he changed into his favourite suit, and when

he reached the dining-room he found that
Mr Leigh had gone so far as to hold up
the meal until he arrived. A cheer greeted
him, and fellows began to fight over his place
at the table. He would sit nowhere but in
his old place between D'Arcy and Telford,
however.

'What did Robson say, Des?'

'Who was the bearded fellow?'

'Was it a damp cellar, old son?'

'Aren't you fagged after walking all that
way?'

'*Where* did you sleep?'

'Why——'

'Shut up!' snapped Desmond as gruffly
as ever, apparently oblivious that he was
some sort of a Lindbergh, or Lawrence of
Arabia. 'I'm going to feed, and it'll be
a poor lookout for anyone who tries to stop
me. There's all afternoon to jaw, but old
Leigh won't let me sit here eating more
than an hour, you funny asses!'

But he was not to escape the lime-light
so easily. His story must have been told
about six or seven times during the afternoon, till he almost had the exact words off
like a recitation. And, of course, as other
fellows repeated it, it grew both in detail
and excitement until, as the incorrigible

D'Arcy said, 'It made Edgar Wallace look pale,' containing sand-bags, chloroform, handcuffs, secret passages, wrecked cars, and quite a number of stolen medallions.

Desmond's father and mother stayed to have tea with the Head-master; and all the time during the meal Desmond's mother sat and looked at her son as if she had never seen him before, and left all the conversation to Dr Newton and the Captain, who managed it very well, and became great friends.

'Well,' said Dr Newton, as they were going at last, 'I suppose I'll see you at the Sports on Wednesday?'

'Of course,' smiled the Captain. 'I want to see how this young rascal runs.'

'Oh, he'd better not be in any races,' murmured Mrs Desmond. 'He must rest——'

'Mother! Mother!' broke in Desmond, forgetting the presence of the Head-master. 'I'm not at all——'

'Perhaps—just *one* race?' smiled the Head-master; and so Mrs Desmond had to give in.

'I'd have liked to introduce you to B. D. Allerick,' said Desmond, as D'Arcy and he escorted his parents to the waiting car; 'but he's bunked off somewhere—he's shy, you know. I'll dig him out on Wednesday for

you, dad. *And* Pat O'Shane. Do be early;
the four-forty first, and I'm jolly well going
to win it.'

By Wednesday the excitement of Desmond's return had died down considerably.
The medallion had been returned to Lord
Inverslowe; Dowling and Robson had been
searched for in vain; Allerick was once more
captain of Wright's, and rapidly recovering
his health and spirits. Things were as gay
as they were at the beginning of the term,
it was as if a cloud had rolled away. Only
one really miserable figure was to be seen
—that of Gregory. Spencer, Collins, and
the others who had been against Allerick
had apologised sheepishly and gone their
usual way; but Gregory had not apologised,
and would not listen to a word against
Robson. Desmond, even when Gregory
accused him of lying, felt sorry for him,
because he felt in the depths of Gregory's
mind was the knowledge that Robson was an
utter cad.

St Martin's field on the Wednesday afternoon was gay with colour and sunshine. All
the fathers seemed so proud, the mothers
so kind, and the sisters so pretty, that
smiles and good humour were the order of
the day.

The final for the four-forty yards, being the first item on the programme, was given an unusual amount of attention, the minds of the spectators being fresh. From the start two figures led, one was the most handsome boy in the School, and one was the most ugly boy. And the handsome boy won, and the ugly boy was second, and the smiling thin Irish chap was third.

What a cheer there was—especially from the flappers—as Desmond turned, breathless and red of face, and received Allerick's hearty slap on the back. Then he looked round to where the other members of the School were congregated, and saw the Wright's House boys waving and shouting. He knew that the feud—the long, bitter, restless feud—was over, and in his excitement he grabbed hold of Allerick's arm and cried, 'It's pax, old man! We've done it! We've done it!'

Allerick understood at once, but he replied, '*You've* done it, Desmond, you mean!'

'Go on! Well, we must make sure that next term a fresh start is made. The two Houses must pull together. Come and meet my pater and mater.—Come on, Pat!'

Desmond always remembered that afternoon as the happiest of his life. The sunshine and the relief of knowing that things were straight again gave it a wonderful glory.

Always he could remember the shadow of the School falling over the vivid green grass, the glaring of the little red flags round the course, the white of the hurdles. He could see Allerick's hot thin face, his tow-like hair standing stiffly up from his forehead, and his crooked smile. He could see D'Arcy's gleaming eyes, and the lazy blue ones of O'Shane; Hare moving seriously and happily around as if he were responsible for every function of the day; and the Tiger running impromptu races on his own, and carrying ices to a small freckled girl in a pale blue frock. He could see the dark shining wave of the Head-master's hair as he moved among the groups of people, chatting and laughing proudly.

But clearest of all he remembered Allerick's face, as for a minute they stood outside the rush and excitement, in the shadow of Leigh's doorway.

'I never saw such a ripping day before,' Desmond said. 'I do hope Leigh's and Wright's will do great things together.'

'Let's hope so—there's plenty of energy to spare now the Houses are friends.'

'And the House-captains,' Desmond retorted, smiling.

Allerick's answering smile assured him that their friendship would be unchanging as the sea which gleamed beyond the playing-fields.

'It's—great . . .' he murmured; and they stood in silence watching the happy crowd.

THE END.